TALKED

to *Death*

LOUISE SHAFFER

BERKLEY PRIME CRIME, NEW YORK

TALKED TO DEATH

A Berkley Prime Crime Book / published by arrangement with the author

PRINTING HISTORY
G.P. Putnam's Sons hardcover edition / September 1995
Berkley Prime Crime mass-market edition / August 1996

The Putnam Berkley World Wide Web site address is
http://www.berkley.com

ISBN: 0-425-15407-6

Berkley Prime Crime Books are published
by The Berkley Publishing Group,
200 Madison Avenue, New York, New York 10016.
The name BERKLEY PRIME CRIME and the
BERKLEY PRIME CRIME design are trademarks
belonging to Berkley Publishing Corporation.

PRINTED IN THE UNITED STATES OF AMERICA

10 9 8 7 6 5 4 3 2 1

For Mom and Roger—
for the same reasons as last time,
plus one more year

Acknowledgments

My thanks to:

Detective Sergeant Al Shepperd, Walter Fee, Sue Castle, John Howland, Martin Berman, José Pretlow, and Iris Torres for help given with generosity and creativity;

the friends who support me: Diana, Debbie, Honey, A. Gin, Bee, Chris and Colin, George and Catherine, and Ellen, who still steps in to bail me out;

and my gratitude to and for: Eric Simonoff, my agent, and Stacy Creamer, my editor. The more I learn about this business, the more I realize how fortunate I am and how special they are.

TALKED
to *Death*

. . . .

Prologue

It wasn't a particularly dramatic scene, as scenes go. There wasn't even a lot of blood—just the dark little trickle that had oozed out of the gunshot wound in the back of the body at my feet. The body that was too still. The dead body. For a second I felt the floor lurch under me. But it quickly settled. I couldn't say the same for my breathing. I forced myself to look up—made myself focus on the white ceiling and the white walls. Anything to keep from seeing what was on the floor.

"Angie?" The voice behind me was so soft I almost couldn't hear it. I turned. Two faces swam before me, the eyes wide with alarm. Mine probably looked the same. From the hallway I thought I heard voices—the voices of my new colleagues, my co-workers on the brand-new job I was so lucky to have. Of course, there was one of their number I'd never get to know. She was the one lying on the rug in front of me.

It was then I realized that to have a murder, there had to be a murderer. From what I already knew of my new companions, there was more than enough motive to go around. So the real question in this particular homicide was not so much whodunit as which one?

1

Now that it's all over, I wish I could say that from the very beginning I sensed on some deep, subconscious level that something wasn't right. A premonition would have been nice. At the very least, I'd like to be able to claim that the reason I gave my agent, Freddie, so much grief about going to Cee Gee Jones's Christmas party was because I had a dark sense of foreboding. But the truth is, I was just being a pain in the ass. Which is something I tend to be when I'm unemployed and trying to find work. Being a pain in the ass keeps me from getting so depressed that all I can do is crawl into bed and pull the covers over my head. Most of the time, Freddie understands.

"Now please, Angela," he said with elaborate patience, "explain again to your poor agent, who you are sending to an early grave from stress, why you do not want to accept an invitation from a woman who is not only the hottest thing happening in television today but the only person in the industry who has shown any interest in hiring you as a producer in five months." As usual, Freddie was conducting his business with me over the phone. He was breathing so heavily, for a moment I really was worried about his stress level. Then an ugly thought occurred to me.

"Freddie, where the hell are you?"

"At the gym," he panted, confirming my suspicion. Like all good agents, Freddie spends his life on the telephone. This used to mean he spent most of his waking hours in his office or lunching in restaurants that were willing to page patrons at their tables. But the flip phone has liberated him. Now he roams the city at will, his cellular lifeline perpetually at his ear. I hate it. I like to know where people are when I'm talking to them.

"If you are on that damn stationary bike . . ."

"Actually, I'm running laps on the track."

"Would it be possible to tone down the heavy breathing? I feel like I'm discussing my career with an obscene caller."

"Can you believe I've knocked off seven pounds and increased my muscle mass by almost three percent?"

"Wow," I said unenthusiastically. I remember the days when true New Yorkers thought exercise, like earthquakes and sushi, was an evil reserved for those inhabiting Southern California. I miss those days.

"About your attendance at Cee Gee's Christmas party . . ." Freddie is not easily distracted.

"I would rather have six months of root canal."

"How about another five months of job search?"

"I don't do talk shows, I do soap operas."

"You used to do soap operas. Now you do the unemployment line."

"Thank you for rubbing it in. Another soap will come along." I said it with a lot more confidence than I felt.

"After the fuss on *Bright Tomorrow,* you're a hard sell, Angie. People think you're difficult."

"I was fired because I refused to do what I believed was wrong for my show. And if you've watched the ratings on

Bright Tomorrow plummet these last three months, you'll have to agree that I—"

Freddie cut me off. "*Liebchen*, nobody cares that you were right. They care that you have a big mouth."

"But look at what happened to the show, dammit."

"You know what I love about you, Angie? After all your years in the business you still believe the work is what matters. It's so cute." Freddie chuckled fondly, then got back to business. "Listen to me carefully, *Liebchen*. You have had three meetings with these people. From what I hear through the rumor mill, they like you. Now they have graciously extended an invitation for which many in our business would cheerfully sell a blood relative. You are to graciously accept. You will attend this soiree."

"I hate industry parties."

"Who doesn't? What's your point?"

"I've heard rumors about Cee Gee's little gatherings. People sit around and ventilate their feelings. You have to communicate, with a capital *C*."

"Not at her Christmas party. Communication is required at the Producer's Brunch and the weekend retreat after the annual Shopping Spree Bonus. However, if they requested that you parade down Broadway naked, at this point in your career it would be something we should consider."

"That is degrading and demeaning."

"There's no business like show business."

"Freddie, have you considered the possibility that they don't really have a job to offer? That they're just jerking us around?"

"No. Whatever gave you an idea like that?"

"They've had one breakfast and two lunches with me, but

we haven't had a meeting at the studio. Every time I've talked to them it starts out like a job interview, but it never goes anywhere. No one discusses the possibility of my joining the team, not even theoretically. And if they're really serious, why haven't they made an announcement about Grace Shipley leaving the show?"

There was a pause on the other end. I knew Freddie was as puzzled about that as I was. For six weeks the village drums had been telling him that Cee Gee Jones, hostess of the superhot, megahit talk show *Cee Gee!*, was looking for a replacement for her longtime friend and senior producer, Grace Shipley. But there had been no face-saving press statement from Ms. Shipley about moving on to new challenges. There hadn't even been the terse citing of creative differences which indicates a bloody parting of the ways accompanied by lawyers and cash settlements. It was as if the firing and hiring process was suddenly caught in some kind of limbo. This apparent dithering seemed strangely out of character for Cee Gee Jones and her first in command, Victoria Townsend-Stuart, who had a reputation for moving quickly and decisively— some said brutally—in such matters.

"No one seems to know exactly what's going on," Freddie admitted finally. "The show has a lot of history with Grace, of course . . ."

"So maybe they're not replacing her, after all."

"No, Cee Gee's determined that it will happen. My sources are very clear on that."

Freddie is plugged into the most reliable gossip in the industry.

"Then I don't get it."

"You don't have to. Just show up at the party. Remember not to wear fur because of the PETA thing, and for God's sake don't let anyone see you eating anything except the crudités. Everyone is counting fat grams this Christmas."

"I don't own a fur and I will not—"

"Sorry, *Liebchen,* got to go. I just saw Mike Rosenthal—the new head guy over at Artists Management. He's on the track ahead of me and I have to network." And so saying, he hung up. Or beamed himself to another planet. Or did whatever the hell you do with a telephone that has an antenna instead of a cord.

Two minutes later, Freddie called back. "That Mike is one terrific human being. We work out with the same trainer, can you believe it?" Since Artists Management is one of the biggest and most powerful talent agencies in the business, I understood how much this trainer connection—however tenuous—meant to Freddie.

"I'm very happy for you. Did you call to share, or was there something else?"

"Just this." His voice got gentle. "I know how you felt about your soap, Angie. And I know how you feel about talk shows. But you're a pro. You realize what working for Cee Gee Jones could do for your career."

"And I don't have to be in love with the job to do it well. I know."

And I tried to believe it. Right up to the very end I tried. I don't care what Freddie says.

At that point, my objection to talk shows was professional, not personal. Like any loyal soap opera employee, I viewed the gab and sleaze fests as the enemy. They were the competition that was running us off the air. Talk is cheap—or at least, it's cheaper to produce than melodrama. And there seems to be no limit to the public's appetite for mothers who have seduced their sons' girlfriends. Or boyfriends.

However, I had to admit that Freddie was right. Despite my unwavering loyalty, I wasn't being swamped with job offers from the few soaps still remaining in New York. And while it was my personal belief that Cee Gee and her cohorts were a passing fancy who would eventually go the way of *Queen for a Day* and *The Gong Show,* at the moment she was the best game in town. And the only one for me, it seemed.

So I'd dutifully done some research on Ms. Jones. It hadn't required much digging. Especially not during the holiday season, when, as usual, Cee Gee's face graced the covers of three national magazines.

The *Ladies' Home Journal* article was a breathless piece about Cee Gee's first Christmas in Connecticut. She'd recently acquired a home in Kent, a town in the trendy northwest corner of the state which is prized as a site for second homes by wealthy Manhattanites who consider themselves too soulful for the Hamptons. "Rustic" and "secluded" are the buzzwords of choice employed by local real estate agents. Every winter the area suffers at least three serious fires started by weekenders in L. L. Bean work boots unacquainted with the intricacies of woodstoves.

I know these things because my sister and her family live in New Milford, a nice, untrendy little community about twenty minutes south of Kent on Route 7. Like most of the other locals, Connie and her family spend a lot of time bitching about the New Yorkers who have brought traffic jams and tortellini salad to what had previously been their exclusive chunk of God's country.

The *Ladies' Home Journal* article was accompanied by a six-page color photo spread of the former farmhouse Cee Gee had just renovated to the tune of eight million dollars. To me, the end result looked as if someone had decided to panel several key rooms of Versailles with barn siding, but then I'm not always *au courant* on interior design.

The shots featuring Cee Gee, her sixteen-year-old daughter, Samantha, and their dog, Hamlet's Violet VI, were actually rather charming. They looked like they were having a genuinely good time trimming the tree and ladling out fat-free eggnog to their neighbors. Especially the dog.

LHJ had scored the major Cee Gee coup of the season with these pictures. *Redbook* had to be content with shots of the same old five-million-dollar penthouse on Park Avenue they'd photographed the year before. And *Family Circle* got stuck covering Cee Gee's annual Christmas show in the TV studio she recently finished building on the New York side of the Hudson River. I'd missed that extravaganza, but from reading the article, I gathered that the event was a Cee Gee tradition. Every year she dismisses her studio audience, and the cameras are hauled into her private, all-white office so that she and her devoted, mostly female staff can don red-and-green lounging clothes and hunker down on oversized cushions in front of a wood-burning fireplace. "We just hang out together and reminisce for the fans at home," Cee Gee was quoted as saying. "It's really just like a wonderful, cozy slumber party with dear friends." It seemed to me that what the dear friends talked about most was Cee Gee. And how generous she was. And kind. And funny. And how much they all loved her. Cee Gee was good for a dozen "Oh, you guys" and bursting into tears.

I had a bad moment realizing that next year I might be the

senior producer responsible for this moment of television history—but I put the thought aside. After all, it wasn't as though
I'd spent the last fifteen years of my life honing the definitive
production of *Uncle Vanya*. I've never been a purist about
artistic standards. I believe in escapist entertainment and I've
always given it my best. So there was no reason for me to be
wandering around my apartment feeling queasy about joining
Cee Gee Jones. And there was even less reason for the big sad
feeling of loss in the pit of my stomach.

The clock over my stove said three to eleven. *Cee Gee!* aired
at eleven in New York. I gritted my teeth and turned on the
tube to watch it—as I had every day since Freddie first alerted
me about the job. After all, I am a pro.

2

The strains of a militantly upbeat theme song flooded my living room as a montage of clips starring Cee Gee at work filled my screen. There she was with her famous blond Dutch bob and her oversized gold hoop earrings. Her mouth, which is a little too thin, was curved in the streetwise grin known on at least three continents; her huge brown eyes sparkled. The woman has the perfect face for her line of work—it's photogenic but not beautiful. Given a session with a good makeup artist, your neighbor could look like Cee Gee Jones. You could look like her. In fact, every Valentine's Day, when her staff does makeovers on selected members of the studio audience, several women do walk away bearing a scary resemblance to their idol.

More important than her look is the instant intimacy she's able to create. Cee Gee bonds—with her guests, her audience, and most of all with the camera. In interviews, she insists that the secret of her success is her honesty. That is why, she claims, her life remains an open book for her fans. As for the PR staff of nine whose job it is to polish and edit that open book for public consumption—well, what do you expect? This is show business.

Like most talk shows, *Cee Gee!* is syndicated. This means the daily segments are taped by an independent production house—in this case Cee Gee's studio—and then sold by a distributor to the networks and cable channels. Very big bucks can be made by a performer whose show is packaged in this manner if he or she can manage to retain a percentage of the action. The piece Cee Gee gouged out of her distributor when she signed on made television history—and won her a permanent slot on all those annual lists of the wealthiest folks in show business. It's to her credit, and the PR team's, that her fans still say they love her because she seems like someone you might meet on line in the supermarket.

On my set, the opening montage of Cee Gee ended and the ensuing long shot came up on her in front of her besotted studio audience, mike in hand.

"Today we're going to talk about women who are addicted to love," she announced, giving the final word a comic reading. Part of her charm is the light touch she brings to her subjects. She has a surprisingly deep, almost masculine voice, with just a trace of her southern roots still in the accent. She plays on this vocal instrument like a virtuoso.

Her guests were a mother, a daughter, and a niece, all of whom seemed to have married a man named Claude. The women—Dawn, Fawn, and Gladys—had alarmingly big hair in identical shades of caramel. Claude was sporting the world's worst toupee. Figuring I'd be bored to tears by this unappetizing quartet, I settled back to watch. But as usual, Cee Gee faked me out. She does have a way of making you care. By the time the first commercial break rolled around, the tissue boxes were out in the studio audience, and I had almost forgotten that I was watching the exploitation of four people whose combined IQ equaled that of a rock.

After the commercial, Cee Gee opened the floor to questions. Since her shows are taped in sequence as if they were live, I assumed that her production staff took advantage of the breaks to do a fast screening of would-be questioners. I wasn't sure exactly how they did it, but I figured there had to be some mechanism for weeding out potential problems.

On this particular day the show was moving along nicely. Cee Gee's audiences know that they are expected to come up with nonjudgmental responses to every situation, no matter how unsavory the guests—"We are here to learn and grow" is one of her favorite admonitions to her followers. Today, all of the questioners were in line with the program. God and divine forgiveness figured prominently in the comments, as did several quotes from a hot new self-help book. One man was moved to cite *Jonathan Livingston Seagull*. I was relieved when no one offered up a selection from *The Prophet*.

As we headed into the home stretch before the credit crawl, Cee Gee looked into the camera to sum up.

"I know you all know what I'm going to say," she said with a self-deprecating little smile. The audience tittered that they did. "Life is about forgiving ourselves. All the pain I see on this show, all the suffering, could be avoided if people could learn to love and heal themselves. I truly believe if nations could do those two things we could achieve lasting peace and end world hunger." The audience gave this sentiment a round of applause. "And now before we close, I have time for one last question . . ." And she leaned down to give the mike to a man seated on the aisle.

That was when it happened. I don't know whether the guy had slipped through the screening process, or had lied about the question he intended to ask.

"If love is all it takes," he snarled, "then what the hell's wrong with your own kid?"

The camera caught Cee Gee as she was in the process of

straightening up. She froze midbend, instant fury flashing in her eyes. The folks in the control booth picked up on it and cut away. But not fast enough for me to miss the look of black hate she shot at the man. Our Lady of the Perpetual Grin had a quick temper, it seemed.

She recovered in a second. "Now go out there and be good to each other," she sang out, giving her fans her signature closing line, and waving jauntily at her close-up camera as if nothing had happened.

But it had. And what I wanted to know was, why had it shown on air? This wasn't live television. Why hadn't somebody edited out that piece of tape in postproduction? The cutting might have been a bit tricky, but that shouldn't have been a problem for a staff as slick as the group behind this show. These people were some of the best in the business. So why hadn't they covered for their star? It was inexcusable. It was the kind of mistake which should cause heads to roll. But of course, a head was scheduled to roll—Grace Shipley's. Or was it? And what about daughter Sam? In the magazine pictures she'd looked like an average teenager—a little bland, but definitely wholesome. So what was going on with her that could make Mommy lose it in front of millions?

3

By the time I arrived at Cee Gee's building for the party that evening, I was cursing Christmas, my agent, and a bus driver named, appropriately, Jesus Fernandez.

If I'm jobless I don't squander my unemployment checks on cabs. I use public transportation. Even if it's four days before Christmas, one of the coldest nights of the year, and I'm wearing my strappy dress sandals with the beading.

When the bus I'd taken reached the stop nearest Cee Gee's apartment building, I almost managed to fight my way through the throng of happy shoppers before Jesus shut the doors. Almost but not quite. Yelling accomplished nothing. Ditto for banging on the door with my bare fists. I was dumped out six blocks away from my destination with no option except to hike back on four-inch heels. I wear these stilts because I'm a little over five feet tall, and no one ever has seen or ever will see me wearing flats. As I limped up Park Avenue I threw in a couple of curses for tall people.

At journey's end I was greeted by a scene of considerable confusion. Cee Gee lives in one of those classy Upper East Side buildings that always remind me of funeral parlors. The doormen are gray-haired and venerable, guests announce themselves in hushed tones, and the mellow lighting drowns the lobby in a sepia wash. The staff in this type of genteel establishment isn't experienced in handling the kind of three-ring circus which occurs when a media star invites two hundred of her closest friends to celebrate the season of joy. Cee Gee's doormen tried to maintain control as a steady stream of limos deposited eager partygoers on the sidewalk under the building canopy, but it was a lost cause. Amid the air kissing and chatter, velum invitations were waved in the general direction of the man who was frantically trying to check off names on a list. Before I lost a couple of toes to frostbite, I began shoving with the rest of the crowd.

Cee Gee's pricey piece of Manhattan real estate accommodated her many guests quite comfortably. It was an apartment with what I believe the decorating experts call "flow." The huge white foyer opened onto a spacious white living room on one side and a spacious white dining room on the other. These two chambers in turn flowed into other chambers, which flowed into still others. It must have required a gut renovation to achieve all that white-on-white dazzle in a conservative old prewar building. There was a lot of glass, and much in the way of mirrors and chrome. Scattered around were pieces of squatty furniture covered with the kind of thin, expensive leather I hate to touch because it reminds me that leather is basically dead skin.

A white curved staircase led to the second story, where, according to *Redbook*, one would find Cee Gee's sleeping quarters and the white marble bathroom with the 180-degree view of the city and the gold swan faucets.

I handed my politically correct cloth coat to someone who insisted that it was his job to hang it up for me, grabbed a glass of champagne from one of the dozens of waiters who seemed to be everywhere, and prepared to be sociable. It was time to party.

The living room was crammed with humans on the make, all trying to appear festive as they jockeyed to connect with someone higher up on the power food chain than themselves. Intense conversations of high-decibel levels were held between people who were busily scanning the room over each other's shoulders. Loud laughter designed to draw attention bounced off the glossy white walls.

I circled the outer perimeter of the room, listening as I went.

". . . a young Helena Bonham Carter for the project . . ." screamed a man with a ponytail and three earrings to a woman wearing a tuxedo.

". . . because we have a relationship with Ovitz, so fuck their relationship . . ." a woman sporting a red rhinestone AIDS ribbon yelled to four guys wearing T-shirts under their dinner jackets.

And it wasn't just a show biz crowd. Cee Gee Jones had the clout to attract an eclectic bunch to her hearth and home. A state senator from somewhere out on Long Island chatted with a woman who had written a best-seller about her sexual encounters in the afterlife, which she experienced for twenty-three minutes following gallbladder surgery. The fashion designer who has done so much to make rich women look like members of an unwashed motorcycle gang hobnobbed with the health guru who has made a fortune touting a tea made from large, flabby mushrooms.

As I watched this swirling humanity, I was suddenly aware that someone was watching me. Directly across from me, framed by a heavily draped floor-to-ceiling window, was Cee Gee's executive producer, Victoria Townsend-Stuart, known to one and all by her boarding school nickname, Townie.

She was standing so still that she could have passed for a piece of sculpture. Only her eyes, ice-blue and fixed on me, seemed to have life. For a brief moment we connected; then without any sign of embarrassment, she looked away and began a slow survey of the room.

As usual, she was dressed in white. Her outfit looked like the sort of getup Maggie Smith wears in Merchant-Ivory films about the good old days with the British upper classes. There was lots of lace, a nipped-in waist, a graceful ankle-length skirt, and a high, ruffled collar. Her thick blond-brown hair was bundled into the upsweep that Charles Dana Gibson made so popular at the turn of the century. On anyone else the look would have been a bit much; Townie got away with it because it was so perfect for her brand of classic, classy beauty. We're talking flawless features, chiseled cheekbones, and the kind of slender figure that used to be described as "willowy." Togged out as she was and standing with the black night of New York behind her, the woman was a knockout.

She was also, if industry gossip was to be believed, the architect of Cee Gee Jones's phenomenal success. And she was reputed to require regular transfusions of ice water to keep her blood circulating.

At that moment something was displeasing her. I followed her frowning gaze to the top of the staircase, where a vision had appeared. Little Sammy was about to make her entrance. In the *Ladies' Home Journal* pictures Samantha had been properly attired in a pleated skirt, blouse, and color-coordinated cardigan. Not so this evening. The correct little schoolgirl had poured herself into a tube of see-through fabric which had molded itself to her body like a coat of paint, leaving nothing to the imagination, including the fact that Cee Gee's baby girl did not believe in underwear. Plunging décolletage revealed a tatoo of a snake slithering across her right breast. For footwear she had chosen a slave bracelet on her left ankle in lieu of shoes.

I figured that the poor kid had to be freezing to death. And seriously pissed off at her mother.

"Not subtle, but quite effective, wouldn't you say?" A voice at my side echoed my thoughts. I turned to see a man with a thatch of silvery hair smiling at me. He was in his sixties, and in a room full of men killing themselves to make a fashion statement, he was an elegant argument for a fine tailor and custom-made shirts.

"Poor baby, she'll never get away with it," he said, indicating Samantha poised at the top of the stairs. "Felice should come along any moment now to . . . Ah yes, there we are." Sure enough, as he spoke, a woman emerged from the throng in the foyer, and quickly mounted the stairs in time to block Samantha's descent.

This time it was the name I recognized, not the face. I hadn't yet met Felice Rovere: Cee Gee's personal assistant, her friend from childhood, and the third member of the trio without whom, Cee Gee regularly informed interviewers with touching modesty, she never could have Made It. The third member of that group was, of course, Grace Shipley. Without whom, it seemed, Cee Gee now could Make It. Maybe.

There was an exchange on the staircase which I couldn't lip-read from where I was standing, but it was obvious that Samantha was outclassed. She turned and went back into the nether regions of the second floor, leaving Felice triumphant in the field.

"Another crisis averted," said my companion. "I'm Mr. Victoria Townsend-Stuart, by the way." Then, as I whipped around to stare at him: "Yes, I know what you're thinking. And you're quite right. In fact, Townie came out with my youngest daughter, Helen."

After that it seemed only civil to introduce myself.

"My name is—" I began, but he cut me off.

"Angela DaVito. I know. Doesn't DaVito translate to 'of life'? I do hope so, because it would suit you admirably."

There was an Alice in Wonderland quality to the conversation that was starting to get on my nerves.

"How do you know my name?"

"I do apologize. It's just that after all the research on you, I feel as if we're old friends."

"What research? What are you talking about?"

"You are, after all, the prime candidate to take over for Grace."

"Me?"

"Yes indeed," said a clear voice behind me.

I turned around to face Victoria Townsend-Stuart. Aka Townie.

4

Mr. Townie leaned across me to give his wife a peck on the cheek.

"Hullo, darling," he said fondly. "Hope you didn't mind my spilling your state secret to Angie."

I had a feeling that she did, but she said, "Nations have state secrets, George. I just produce a talk show."

She had a lovely voice. I'd noticed it during our previous meetings. It was a singer's voice. Light soprano was my guess. At some point in her life she'd trained hard to achieve it. She gave me a smile. "Please forgive George. He reads too many novels about British spies in World War Two. Have you spoken to Cee Gee yet this evening, Angie? I know she wants to talk to you."

"I just got here—I haven't seen Cee Gee yet."

"I'll take you to her." She put a gentle hand on her husband's arm. "Do stay out of trouble, George."

He smiled affably. "Always, darling," he said. But she'd already turned and begun moving so quickly through the crowd that I had to scramble after her. She led the way through two more dazzling white rooms with off-white accents. Here and there the monotony was broken by splashes of crimson. I remembered reading somewhere that crimson was Cee Gee's favorite color. It bothers me to realize how much I retain about people in my business who don't really interest me.

As I followed Townie, I reviewed the portions of the Cee Gee Jones story I knew. She'd been a troubled kid growing up on the wrong side of the tracks in a small town somewhere in the South. She dropped out of school at sixteen, and was pregnant and unmarried by the time she was twenty-two. The birth of Samantha had brought on an epiphany resulting in her heroic return to high school. After which she attended college, majoring in journalism just long enough to drop her southern twang and acquire mid-Atlantic speech patterns. She left academia when she landed her first job at a local television station near the school. All these facts had been chronicled in her inspirational memoir *Reinventing Myself: A Woman's Story*. The book was rumored to be the first of a trilogy.

I also knew that Victoria Townsend and Cee Gee Jones had met on the job when Cee Gee was hosting a talk show in a smallish market in Georgia. Townie was a Yankee import from a fine old New York family, working in the South on her first producing job.

"I knew from the very beginning down in Georgia that Townie was the right producer for me. She understood that I must follow my own inner mission," Cee Gee had told an interviewer.

"Grace was working at the same station down there, and that was when she joined us. Later we were blessed again when my oldest and dearest friend, Felice Rovere, came to be with us in New York. I couldn't have made it without all three of them."

As we maneuvered our way through the crowd, people came up to Townie to talk, but she managed to get away from them without breaking stride. She seemed to melt away, leaving the person who'd approached her smiling at empty air.

Only once did she allow herself to be stopped—by two bright-faced kids in their twenties.

"Angie, I'd like you to meet two of the talented young people who work for us," she said graciously. "David was an intern, but we've discovered that he has a real gift for comedy. He's been doing the audience warm-up before the show for the past two months."

David, who was cute as a button, shot me a flirty grin. He was a perfect choice to work a studio full of female tourists from the heartland. The girl with him had the air of an eager puppy. Her hair was swept up on top of her head and she was dressed in white lace.

"And this is Peggy Lawton," said Townie. "She came to us as a receptionist and is rapidly making herself invaluable as my office assistant. She helped put this party together."

"It's just been so much fun," the girl gushed. "And of course, I did get to play hooky from the studio for the whole day." She giggled.

Meanwhile David had picked up on my name. "Are you Angela DaVito?" he asked enthusiastically. "We've all been wondering about you."

I was about to ask him who "we" was and why they were wondering about me, when I felt Townie doing her melting act at my side. I murmured goodbyes and took off after her. I was being uncharacteristically docile—follow the leader has never been my favorite game, unless I'm the one doing the leading—and it disturbed me. I hadn't realized until then just how badly I wanted to work again.

———

At the back of the apartment we climbed a narrow staircase to the second floor. On one side was an impressive wrap-around terrace. On the other was a short corridor which led to more rooms. Townie opened a door and we walked into what I assumed was the office.

If Cee Gee's public spaces were marked by a chilly *Architectural Digest* chic, her private quarters were pure MGM, circa 1930. Her office boasted padded silk walls, carpet that climbed up to meet them, gold wall sconces, and a white and gold wedding cake of a desk. The place cried out for a number by Fred and Ginger.

However, the only person in the room was the mistress of the house, who was wearing an elaborately draped gown which would have been fantastic on someone with the height to carry it. I think it's supposed to be a part of Cee Gee's appeal that she never looks quite right in the wildly expensive designer clothes she adores. She didn't hear us come in because she was facing away from the door, talking on a gold and white phone.

"I don't care what the fucking co-op rules are," she shouted into the receiver. "Some schmuck sent my security guards away. I hired those people for the lobby because I need them." The person on the other end then voiced a response which caused her to explode with, "Because I am a goddamn fucking star, you idiot. Because there is a person out there who wants to—"

"Cee Gee!" Townie's voice rang out clear and authoritative. Cee Gee turned and realized that she was not alone. She took a deep breath and spoke quietly and quickly into the receiver. "I am going to call the security systems people. I am going to tell them that you made a mistake. Then they are going to send over more guards and you are going to see to it that those guards guard me and my guests. Understood?"

She hung up and treated me to the famous grin.

"Angie, welcome. Sorry about the fuss. This is a very old-fashioned building and they don't seem to understand some of the special needs we have."

I wondered if the "we" was editorial, royal, or just-us-girls.

"I'm so glad you could come tonight," she added as she came forward, her hand extended.

Before I could shake it, we heard screams.

Cee Gee and Townie looked at each other.

"Sammy," said Cee Gee.

"The bedroom," said Townie.

I started running because they did.

5

Cee Gee's bedroom featured more white-on-white, and a bed swathed in a tent of gauzy net. But no Sammy. Then a light went on in the bathroom and we raced to open the door.

My first thought was that the decorator had overdone the crimson-accent splashes. Then I heard Townie's sharp intake of breath. Samantha, who was standing by the light switch, said shakily, "It's bleeding."

But the stuff on the walls was much too red. I'd have fired a makeup artist who couldn't mix better fake blood than that.

"Jesus Christ," said Cee Gee. She was looking up at the light fixture, from which a large doll was strung up in a noose. By large I mean about three feet high. It was wearing gold hoop earrings and a blond Dutch bob, and its plastic lips were twisted in a familiar grin. All in all, not a bad likeness of Cee Gee Jones.

"What the hell is going on here?" demanded a voice from the doorway. The accent was one I still associate with George Wallace and people who hold lynchings—forget all those articles about the New South in *Time*. We all turned to see Felice.

"People are asking— Holy shit," she said as she caught sight of the hanging figure. "I told you we should have gotten rid of that damn thing, Cee Gee. It always gave me the creeps."

Felice approached the doll. I think she was going to grab it, but before she had a chance, it twisted where it hung.

In the center of its chest a hole had been cut. In the hole someone had rammed a toy bullet. Fake blood dripped down from the "wound." Felice stepped back fast.

We all stared at the thing in silence. Then Townie, Felice, and Samantha moved as if by instinct to surround Cee Gee.

"Are you all right?" Felice asked her.

"I'm sorry, Mama," said Samantha. "I shouldn't have let it freak me out."

"No, you shouldn't," said Townie. "You've already caused enough trouble as it is."

Samantha reacted as if she'd been slapped. "It was dark when I came in—I didn't know what the fuck it was."

Townie gave her the kind of look most people reserve for things covered with slime. "It would be so nice if you had the grace not to whine," she said.

"Stop blaming me for all of it," Samantha said. "Because it isn't my fault. It wasn't my idea for you to—"

"Sammy!" Felice warned at the same time that Townie said harshly, "That's enough."

But it was Cee Gee who stopped Samantha by stroking her face gently and crooning, "It's okay, baby. No one blames you. Do we, Townie?"

The words were gentle too but there was a hardness in the look she gave Townie which didn't allow for disagreement.

Townie paused before answering. "No one is blaming anyone."

It was obviously a major capitulation and it melted Samantha's defiance. "I'm sorry, Mama," she whispered. "I'm so sorry."

Clearly we were no longer talking about the scream in the bathroom. I wondered again what the hell the kid had done— or hadn't done.

Townie turned away in disgust.

"How many people heard?" she asked Felice.

"Everyone in the foyer."

"And you chose to exacerbate their curiosity by racing up here. Brilliant."

Felice flushed. "I thought—" she began, but Townie cut her off.

"Don't. Thinking is not one of the things you do well. Stick to that for which you have some aptitude—if there is such a thing."

Felice's face, which was already a dark red, got darker. As the two women faced each other they presented an interesting contrast. One was delicate steel; the other was salt of the earth. Felice had a large, good-natured face, with big features and eyes so brown they seemed black. Her beautifully tailored dinner suit was black, and her dark hair was cut into one of those short, expensive wedges you get in salons where the owner's first name doubles as the title of the establishment. And Felice Rovere was serious about jewelry. In quantity. Diamonds seemed to be her gem of choice, but emeralds ran a close second. I'm not a connoisseur but I'd have been willing to bet every sparkly carat was real.

Although Townie had a couple of inches on her, Felice was by far the sturdier of the two. If she ever lost control and initiated the slugfest I felt she craved, my money would have been on her. But in this contest of wills she wasn't even a serious contender. After a moment she shrugged and turned away.

"Stay with Samantha until she has pulled herself together," Townie said to her. "Cee Gee, you come downstairs with me."

"I'm okay," said Samantha.

"You don't look it. Make her presentable, Felice. Then come downstairs as quickly as possible." She looked at the walls. "First you'd better get rid of this mess. God knows who might come up here to use the bathroom." She started for the door, with Cee Gee dutifully trailing behind her.

"Wait a minute," I heard myself say. "Don't you want to report this to the police?"

All three women turned to stare at me as if I'd dropped in from another universe. I was aware that Samantha was looking at me too, but for different reasons, I thought. It was Townie who finally broke the silence. "That won't be necessary," she said carefully.

"Angie, why don't you go downstairs with Cee Gee and Townie?" Felice offered.

When I was in grammar school there was always a bunch of little girls who had secrets, which they used to make everyone else feel like outsiders. I used to loathe them when I was six, and I hadn't changed much over the years.

"I hate to be a sissy, but doesn't it strike you that this is the action of someone who is feeling just a tad hostile? To say nothing of overwrought? I know we don't like to dwell on it, but there are a lot of crazies watching the tube these days. If I were you, I'd want to know who did this, and if God talks to them when they turn on the toaster oven."

Something which sounded like a stifled snicker came from Samantha. The other three exchanged a glance that was so quick it almost didn't happen. Again it was Townie who spoke.

"Angie, the truth is, we know who did this," she said. "And I assure you that this"—she gestured toward the spattered walls as she searched for the right word—"this prank does not represent a physical threat to anyone. However, it is a part of an unpleasant situation which could have a negative impact on Cee Gee's image if it became public, so we don't want to involve the authorities. I'm sure you can understand."

Well, I could, and I couldn't. On the one hand, Cee Gee's image was the cornerstone of all their shiny success. On the other hand . . .

"Who did it?" I asked.

"It's too long a story to go into at the moment," said Townie.

"Although we certainly do owe you an explanation after all of this," Cee Gee added with a genuinely sweet smile. "We will fill you in on the details, I promise."

"But right now we must go downstairs," said Townie. "There are too many creative people with active imaginations down there."

She was right about that. After Samantha's vocal pyrotechnics they had to do some damage control.

I want to think that's why I did what I did next. I want to believe that my producer's instincts kicked in and I automatically went into crisis mode. What I don't want to believe is that I did it because I wanted to toe the line. I'd rather not think I was that desperate for a job.

"Why don't the three of you go downstairs?" I suggested. "I'll stay here with Samantha and we'll see what we can do about cleaning up."

"No, I can—" Felice began, but Townie stopped her.

"What a wonderful idea, Angie. Thank you." She was looking at me happily. I had the feeling that I'd passed some kind of test. All three women started for the door; then Townie turned. "I know I don't have to tell you not to mention this to anyone," she said.

"Of course not."

"And if you can manage to stay after the party tonight, I'm sure we can sort out all of this." So saying, she bestowed another of her smiles on me and left with Felice and Cee Gee following close behind.

As the bedroom door closed, Samantha turned to me. "Nice save," she said with a sour look. "You really do know how to kiss ass."

Since I'd just been accusing myself of doing that very thing, she'd hit a nerve.

6

"I think you'd better explain that," I said evenly. Samantha stared back at me just as evenly. She wasn't a raving beauty, but the *Ladies' Home Journal* layout hadn't done her justice. She had one of those faces the camera doesn't flatter. Samantha had apple cheeks, a round little nose, and her mother's mouth. Her hair was dark brown and her eyes were the same color and shape as Cee Gee's. But there the resemblance stopped. Cee Gee may have been the adult, but she didn't have the tough, knowing look I saw in her daughter's eyes.

"In what way am I kissing ass?" I asked.

"Forget it."

"You said it. You should be able to back it up."

"Hey, nobody listens to what I say. Nobody gives a shit what I think."

"I don't believe that."

But I did. Samantha was one of those people who don't command attention. You often find that in the children of celebrities. The parent has charisma to burn; the kid is charismatically challenged. And it's not just a parent-child thing. My sister Connie has star quality and I don't. It made me feel a certain kinship with the sullen kid standing in front of me.

"I have a feeling you're smart," I said. "Especially when it comes to people. And you don't say things you don't mean."

She assessed me for a moment. Then she shrugged. "You want to work for them, so you're bailing them out. It's a good move. Townie loves all that happy horseshit about teamwork and pulling together. I think it reminds her of the dear old days when she was head girl for her school dorm."

"Are you saying that cleaning up this bathroom will get me a job as senior producer?" I said it like I seriously doubted it, although I knew people in the industry who had been hired for crazier reasons.

"Well, she's real sure about your loyalty now."

"And she wasn't before?"

"It could have gone either way. You protected that actress on your show, which was good. But you did work with the cops."

"Townie knows about that?"

"Who doesn't?"

Well, I have to admit that I was pleased. Because my little outing with the police was one of my proudest moments. It happened when I was working on *Bright Tomorrow;* there had a been a murder in the studio and I'd helped figure it out. Actually, to be completely honest, I didn't merely *help*—I was downstage center solving the sucker. It impressed the hell out of me that I was able to do that, and it was gratifying to hear that my fame had spread. But why had that been a problem for Townie?

"So the fact that I've been involved with the police was a strike against me?"

"I thought you were going to blow the gig when you started in about Mama talking to them. I should have known you'd back off." She sounded as if in some way I'd betrayed her.

"Why does that make you so angry? Do you want someone to go to the police, Samantha?"

That threw her. "Me? Why should I want that?"

"Maybe because you're worried about your mother. And you think the cops could help."

Suddenly she looked her age.

"If you want to tell me about it . . ."

For a moment I thought she might. But then she remembered how tough she was. "There's nothing to tell," she said. "Mama's fine and Townie's got everything under control."

"I don't think you believe that."

"Hey, I don't know shit about anything. I'm just the spoiled-brat kid who makes trouble."

"Is that according to Townie or Felice?"

"What the fuck is that supposed to mean?"

"Just that I have the feeling you're working overtime to drive somebody nuts and I don't think it's your mother."

Stony silence. Deadpan stare. I tried a long shot.

"Or is it Grace Shipley you don't like?"

Bull's-eye. Her face went bright red and blotchy. She had that kind of complexion. If she were one of the kids acting on a show of mine, I'd recommend a light beige foundation to smooth it out.

"Gra . . ." She stopped because she was having trouble getting the name out, and started again. "Grace is a brass-bound bitch," she managed.

"Why? What did she do to you?" Or what did you do to her, would have been my next question. But Samantha had suddenly realized that she'd said too much.

She flashed me a big phony smile. "Grace never did anything to me," she said brightly. "You're right, sometimes I say shit just to make everybody crazy. You've got to clean that frigging bathroom. Want help?"

She was determined to change the subject. I decided not to push.

"You don't have to go in there," I said. "It seemed to upset you pretty badly."

"I can handle it." But I noticed she wasn't moving toward the bathroom.

"Why don't I get started first? You can stand in the doorway and keep me company." I walked briskly into the bathroom and began fiddling with the cord that was tied around the doll's neck. It was a heavy grade of household twine. I'd used some exactly like it when I was tying up the box of Christmas presents I always mail to my cousins in New Jersey so I won't have to visit them and hear little Angela play "Adeste Fideles" on the accordion. She also does "Granada."

As I fooled around with the knot I heard Samantha draw in another deep breath behind me. Quickly, to distract her, I asked, "Where did this doll come from? Didn't I hear Felice say it belongs to your mother?"

"It was one of Grace's big ideas. She had it made. Well, really it was this guy she was tangled up with who did it. It's a prototype for a Cee Gee doll."

"You mean this is supposed to be a toy for children?"

Samantha nodded. "Townie backed her, of course. Townie always backs . . . always backed Grace. No matter what crap she came up with," she added bitterly.

I eased the noose over the doll's head.

"The idea was that Mama should put out a Cee Gee Jones doll. So they hired Grace's stud and he spent tons of money showing the fucker to toy companies. I could have told them how stupid it was. Little girls don't watch Mama's show."

That made sense to me. I wondered why Grace hadn't seen it. And more to the point, why Townie had backed her.

"Isn't it awfully big?"

"That's the one they used in the display. The real thing

was supposed to be much smaller. Which was also a shitty idea."

I'd gotten the doll loose, put it on the floor, and was trying to wipe off the fake blood.

"I mean why try to sell a doll that's one size when you plan to make one that's smaller?" she asked.

"Did they ever find a buyer?"

"Are you kidding? Someone did some market research and figured out what I could have told them all along. It really pissed me off. They spent a lot of Mama's money on bullshit for no reason except Grace had the hots for a loser who dumped her six months later. Grace's crotch cost Mama a lot over the years."

"And now they're firing her."

Once again she realized she'd been talking too much. "Shit, I don't know what that's all about," she said, doing her best to look innocent. It was a mistake. Innocent was not her forte.

I stopped dabbing at the mess on the doll and turned to look at her. "You care a lot about your mother, don't you, Samantha?"

The tears welled up so fast she didn't have time to blink. "Some people would tell you I'm the worst problem she's got," she said huskily.

"I don't buy that."

There was a pause while we looked at each other. Then she walked bravely into the bathroom and picked up one of her mother's white monogrammed washcloths.

"Let me give you a hand," she said.

So the girlish confidences were over. Just as well, I told myself. After all, I wanted to work for these people, not investigate them.

At that point, it was the truth. More or less.

It didn't take much to get rid of the fake blood. It was a standard mix from the smell: Karo syrup, cornstarch, and food coloring. There were no fancy ingredients like glycerine or K-Y Jelly which would have caused real cleaning problems.

According to Samantha, the doll usually sat on the couch in her mother's office at the studio. She had no idea how it got over to Park Avenue. "Mama never locks her office door at the studio, so anyone could have taken it" was the best she could offer.

After we'd cleaned up as much as we could, Samantha announced, "I gotta get into the fucking dress Townie wants me to wear." With that, she went off, leaving the doll and me on our own.

I studied the doll for a few seconds. Although she looked better than she had, there was still that nasty hole in the chest. Stashing her out of sight would require opening closets and drawers which were not mine. Instead of resorting to that, I undressed her, draped her in a rakish white towel, and settled her on the bathroom clothes hamper. Not bad, but something seemed to be missing. I spied Cee Gee's monogrammed white shower cap and put it on her head at a jaunty angle. Perfect. As I stepped back to admire my handiwork a glowering Samantha reappeared. She was wearing a blue velvet number with a dropped waist, puffed sleeves, and a lace collar. On a slender, fair-skinned blonde—a young Townie, for instance— it would have been swell. It made Samantha look like a girl whose social life consisted of doing other kids' homework. She gave me a look.

"Townie is a total asshole," she said.

On that note we marched off to rejoin the festivities.

7

Felice swooped down on us as we hit the staircase and whisked us off to a corner, where she filled us in, sotto voce, on the details of Operation Cover-up.

"Now, if anybody asks you about that scream, you just tell them that Cee Gee accidentally locked herself on the terrace. She called out for help when she saw Angie and Townie. Townie let Cee Gee out and then Angie stayed upstairs to powder her nose in the bathroom—which I pray to the Lord looks better now. Angie met up with Samantha in the hallway and you both came downstairs together. We all think the whole thing is very funny, especially Cee Gee. . . . Did you get that damn bathroom cleaned up?"

"Yes," said I.

"Thank you, Jesus," she said, and plunged back into the crowd. Samantha slouched off to be rude to her mother's guests, and I was on my own again. I'm not sure why parties always bring out the shy violet in me; perhaps it has something to do with having spent my adolescence with an older sister who was not only gorgeous but gifted with perfect pitch and a vocal range of four octaves. Maybe it was all those years I spent looking like a dead ringer for my Uncle Paulie the bookie, before Paulie went on to that great racetrack in the sky and left me a small inheritance which I invested in a nose job. Whatever. I roamed around feeling awkward until I finally wound up at the buffet table. I went for the crudités platter— let Freddie try to claim I don't follow orders—and helped myself to a dab of some greenish paste that looked like it was full of fiber.

Meanwhile everybody else was working the room. Even Samantha had gotten herself into a conversation with a man old enough to be, if not her father, a young uncle. They were seated on a sofa and her body language as she curved toward him could only be described as deeply, seriously sexy. Given the blue velvet schmatte, it was a real feat.

I turned back to the buffet table, hoping to find something a little less chewy, and saw that I wasn't the only one who was noticing Samantha's performance. Standing about three feet away from me was that eager girl, Peggy Lawton. She looked a lot less chipper than she had earlier—obviously she'd been doing KP, and she wasn't dressed for it. Her upswept hair was sliding off the top of her head, and there was a green stain on one side of her lacy white skirt. I thought I recognized the stuff I'd been attempting to swallow. She was staring at Samantha, who was now allowing her fingers to brush her swain's knee. A look I couldn't quite read crossed Peggy's face. Her whole body seemed to sag as if suddenly she'd gotten very tired. As I watched her it occurred to me that she was only a few years older than Samantha. I wondered just how much she envied the boss's daughter.

Just then she seemed to remember where she was. She squared her shoulders with a jerk, did some kind of interior mental fluff-up, and pasted her perky smile back in place. Personally, I've always felt perkiness was a trait best left to toy poodles. But I'm probably in the minority on that one.

———

At that moment, the adorable David approached Peggy.

"Hey," he said, giving her what had to be the most devastatingly smoky glance in his repertoire. "Are you going to work all night?"

It was a wasted effort. "Looks like it," she said.

"What a waste of a good party. You should play more."

Peggy began stacking dirty plates on a tray. "I'm afraid I'll have to leave the playing to you," she said cheerfully. "I don't have time."

"Let me take those plates into the kitchen for you and we'll go somewhere and play together."

"David," she said gently, "you wouldn't enjoy the kitchen. People are sweating in there." She patted his cheek. "But thanks anyway. Now, you'd better go somewhere and be charming." She hefted the tray in a manner that suggested she'd done more than a little waitressing in her time, and bore it off to the kitchen. David looked after her in astonishment. Clearly he couldn't believe that any female with functioning brain synapses would turn him down.

The party continued rolling along until eleven o'clock. Then it was as if someone had given a signal. Everyone started to leave. It amazed me. I don't entertain much because it means using my kitchen for more than making coffee, but on the rare occasions when I do throw a party, my guests don't troop out together in an orderly group in time for me to get my beauty sleep. There's always someone who wants to tell one more Katharine Hepburn story, or, if it's been that kind of evening, to sing yet another chorus of "Send In the Clowns."

Cee Gee's guests were better trained. In twenty minutes the apartment had emptied of everyone except Cee Gee, Felice, Townie, George, Samantha, me, and the caterer's staff. Fifteen minutes later the hired hands marched out the door. I noticed that Peggy was among them. She'd obviously decided to stop kidding herself that she was a guest and had changed into a practical T-shirt-and-jeans ensemble for the kitchen cleanup. Gone was the fancy hairdo; her party finery had been packed away in the large black garment bag she'd slung over her shoulder. She looked decidedly unperky. I felt sorry for her as she trudged off into the night.

I'd been invited, as promised, to hang with Cee Gee et al. So after Samantha went off to bed, the rest of us retired to the Rogers and Astaire Memorial Office, where what I had a feeling was a well-practiced routine took place. First Cee Gee, Felice, and Townie removed their shoes. Cee Gee and Felice kicked off theirs, Townie stepped carefully out of hers. Then Cee Gee flopped on one sofa, while Felice sprawled on another. Townie settled into a large armchair opposite them and tucked her feet daintily under her. George, who kept his shoes on, retreated to a corner of the room. From the inner recesses of his impeccable suit he produced several pages of what I thought I recognized as *The Racing Form* from my days with Uncle Paulie. I perched on the corner of a tufted satin ottoman and wondered where Grace used to sit.

"What a night," sighed Cee Gee. "I told you we should have stuck with our old caterer. What was that green shit?"

"Dried celery pâté," said Felice. "There's tons of it left."

"I'll bet."

"I'll have the maid pack it up and take it over to the homeless shelter first thing in the morning," said Felice. "At least we'll get a tax deduction out of it. And when the thank-you flowers come in tomorrow, I—"

"Felice, could we skip your domestic arrangements, fascinating though I'm sure they are?" asked Townie. "I'd like to get to bed before one, and George isn't as young as he used to be."

From across the room George blew her a kiss.

"Besides, I'm sure Angie is dying of curiosity," Townie added.

"Of course she is—how terrible we're being," said Cee Gee, and sat up. Felice swung her feet off the coffee table. I felt the atmosphere in the room change from slumber party to summit meeting.

Cee Gee took the floor. She leaned forward and fixed me with an earnest gaze. "Angie, before you can understand what happened tonight, you need a little background." She did the famous grin. "Now that our new studio is finished, we are about to start a time of growth and change. This is the way it must be. I know it, here." She gestured to the same general area of her anatomy where her namesake doll had taken the hit from the toy bullet. "I always listen to my inner voice. That's why I've been so successful. I believe we're always rewarded when we follow our mission and do what we've been put on this planet to accomplish."

It seemed to me that a hallelujah was called for—or at the very least an amen—but I wasn't about to go first.

"However, growth means losing as well as gaining," Cee Gee continued. "Losing can be a good and cleansing part of the process. But not everyone is able to accept that truth. So when we had to decide that Grace Shipley really couldn't be a part of our new adventure . . . well, I'm afraid she took it rather badly."

My sympathies were with Grace. I also get testy when I'm dumped. And I'd really be cross if someone tried to tell me it was a spiritual thing.

"Why was it necessary to . . . uh . . . let Grace go?" I figured that the situation was a bit too exalted for the word "fire."

"We want to branch out into some new areas," said Townie. "Grace is simply not equipped to handle the work."

So much for the golden team Cee Gee touted in her interviews.

"And she chose to see this 'letting go,' as you put it so perfectly, as a rejection," said Cee Gee. "So she's been acting out in a variety of ways. Like making that scene in the bathroom."

"Grace Shipley whipped up the Friday the thirteenth number?"

"It was just another expression of her pain. It's so sad." But Cee Gee didn't sound sad. If anything, I'd have said the idea of Grace's pain made her a happy camper.

"How did she do it? Did she just turn up at the door carrying a doll the size of a toddler, and a couple of pints of fake blood? Someone must have seen her."

"This has been a busy day—everyone has been in and out, getting ready for the party. And Grace has her own key to my apartment. As do Felice and Townie, of course."

"And a grown woman pulled that stunt to get back at you? An adult with a successful career did that because you fired her?"

"Without Cee Gee, Grace isn't going to have a career," drawled Felice. "Not when the rest of the industry finds out what a terrible—"

"Unfortunately Grace isn't a very stable person," Townie broke in hurriedly. "That's the main reason I haven't let her go before this. Grace has never been up to our standard. But I've always been afraid of what she might do if we dropped her."

"She needs help," Cee Gee chimed in. "And we have to hope she'll get it."

All three of them nodded again.

Bull, I thought.

Maybe what I couldn't swallow was the notion that Townie, the poster child for ice maidens, would be squeamish about firing anyone. Or maybe it was because I felt that underneath all the New Age compassion, they all disliked Grace Shipley a lot. Whatever, I just didn't trust them.

If Freddie had been there he would have told me to hell with trust, just keep my mouth shut. These are potential employers, he would have said. Thank them for lying to you, go home, pray they liked you enough to call your agent with a two-year deal, and stop with the questions. And Freddie would have been absolutely right.

So naturally I said, "There's something I don't understand. You told me earlier that this situation could reflect badly on Cee Gee's image—I assume you meant the fact that you're firing Grace. Why would that be a problem?"

"It's rather complicated," said Townie.

"Why?"

For a second I thought no one had an answer, but Felice stepped in. "Cee Gee's always been too quick to hand over the glory to everybody else. She let the fans think Grace did a lot more than she really did. And now they'll think it's real disloyal for Cee Gee to be firing her."

"She'd been threatening to show up at the party tonight,"

said Cee Gee. "That was why I wanted extra security. We were afraid that in her despair she might make a scene." She sighed. "Poor Grace. I believe we should stay in touch with the feelings of our inner child, but that doesn't mean we must act on those feelings."

That bit of wisdom seemed to wrap up the session as far as my companions were concerned. They all began putting on their shoes. Simultaneously. In his corner, George rose, stuffed an envelope with *The Racing Form* and what I assumed was his list of picks, and strolled over to Cee Gee. There was a gleam in his eye as he held out the envelope and said casually, "See to it that Al gets this tomorrow, would you, Cee Gee?"

Across the room Townie was instantly on alert. "George, please," she said in a warning tone. I could tell he heard her, but he was having too much fun annoying Cee Gee, who had stiffened in disapproval.

"You know I feel that Al has an addictive personality," she said icily. "I should think you'd have better things to do than to corrupt my doorman."

"Ah, dear Cee Gee," he said. "It is always a treat to watch you enact righteous indignation—it's one of your best poses."

"What the hell does that mean?" Cee Gee demanded.

"Nothing," said Townie hastily. "George, would you tell Pavel we want the car?" She opened her turn-of-the-century white lace evening bag, pulled out a sleek little cellular phone Freddie would have coveted, and handed it to him. The move struck me as one a mother might make pulling out a toy to distract a wayward child. I wondered how much time she spent playing buffer between her star and her husband. George took the phone and winked broadly at me.

When we were finally in the elevator, heading for the lobby, Townie turned to her unrepentant spouse.

"Really, George," she said.

"You mustn't frown, Victoria," he said tenderly. He reached over and gently traced a tiny line between her brows. "How many times must I tell you it will cause wrinkles?"

If it had been me, and if I'd been as pissed off as I sensed she was, I would have slugged him. But to my surprise a reluctant smile tugged at her mouth.

"You're incorrigible, George," she said.

"Perhaps. But you mustn't begrudge me my bit of fun, darling." He kissed her cheek, and we finished our trip downward in silence.

In the lobby, he gave the envelope to the doorman with instructions to pass it on to Al.

8

Fortunately Freddie is not the kind of man to carry a grudge. I guess it would be impossible given his life's work. The next morning he was on the phone at the crack of dawn. Actually it was nine-fifteen, but any time before noon is the middle of the night to me. It's a holdover from my childhood when I was the younger half of the Singing DaVito Sisters and Mama was booking our act into the better Elks clubs and American Legion posts throughout New England. We seldom got to bed before midnight, which played havoc with our REM cycles, but Mama figured we had to make sacrifices for our art—and her dreams.

All of which is by way of explaining why I was not at my best when Freddie called me.

"Splash some cold water on your face and listen to me, *Liebchen*," he commanded. "We have an offer from *Cee Gee!*" He then proceeded to outline a deal which was better than any I'd been offered before.

"Take it," I said.

The silence on the other end told me how deeply I'd injured him. "I'm going to pretend you didn't say that, Angie," he said at last. "As if I'd ever let you take a first offer. Besides, guess who's going to be negotiating for them. Dave Rothstein, that's who. Can you believe it? Me and Dave?"

I guess for an agent it was the equivalent of going one-on-one with Michael Jordan. Or single-handedly taking on all the bulls at Pamplona.

"Congratulations, Freddie. Enjoy."

"I'll call you when I've got something to report."

"I'll be waiting."

"No point in you sticking around the apartment. Go shopping. Have lunch. This may take some time." It was part of our ritual for Freddie to say this. We both knew I'd be glued to the phone while he and strangers decided my fate.

"Will do," I lied. That was my part of the ritual.

By three o'clock that afternoon Freddie had bumped up my salary and upgraded my spot on the credit crawl. By five o'clock I was the new senior producer of *Cee Gee!* In the morning I was to report to Cee Gee's studio for a briefing with Townie. However, I would not begin work officially until after the first of the year.

"You mean I'm actually going to have a meeting in an office instead of a restaurant?" I asked. "I'm not sure I'll know how to act if someone named Teddy isn't reciting the chef's specials."

"Angie, will you lighten up? This is one hell of a way to start off the new year. I'm very proud of you."

"Thanks," I said, wondering why I wasn't.

Freddie and I made a date for our celebratory lunch at the Russian Tea Room, which was the final phase of our getting-Angie-a-job ritual. After hanging up, I could feel depression settling over me like a low-lying cloud.

I nuked some Lean Cuisine lasagna, which is what I do when I have to cook, and started wandering around my apartment. I like to characterize my home as cozy, although my sister Connie informs me that "scuzzy" would be the *mot juste*. I will admit that maintaining the building is not high on my landlord's list of priorities. The boys at Bascoom Realties are still sulking because our tenants union blocked their attempt to convert the property to a co-op during the Reagan greed years. They paint our apartments when forced to by the law and our lawyer, using a product which looks like, and covers our walls as well as, skim milk. They have not yet repaired the security intercom since it went out during the late sixties. No one has been able to place the native tongue of the last three superintendents they hired, all of whom have left us in the dead of night, handcuffed and screaming the words "political asylum."

I live happily in this marginal slum on the Upper West Side. My furniture consists of thrift shop specials and the rejects I scavenged off the streets before I started making a living wage. In recent years I've had everything refinished and reupholstered for a price that was only slightly higher than what it would have cost me to start over. On my sofa I keep the collection of teddy bears our fans sent to Connie and me during our winter as the stars of *Uncle Beano's Radio Hour*. The doll Uncle Beano gave me for Christmas sits on the bookcase with the scrapbooks of clippings Mama collected when we were performing.

I hadn't looked at those scrapbooks in twenty years, but suddenly I found myself pulling them off the shelf. I sat cross-legged on the floor and started going through them.

Connie always hated show business, but I would have crawled over hot coals to stay in it. Which was too bad because Connie was the talent. When she walked I nearly starved to death trying to make it as an actress on my own.

The turning point came for me when I was working as an extra on the soap opera *Bright Tomorrow.* The leading lady, an actress named Jesse Southland, suggested that perhaps a career behind the scenes might be a better choice. She offered to help me get started as a producer.

It was the best thing that ever happened to me. Once I started I went up the ranks quickly, until I became the executive producer of the show. I loved my crew, loved my actors, loved being in charge. I put together the show I'd have wanted to act for if I'd had the gift. My career on *Bright Tomorrow* made me successful, fulfilled, and solvent.

And it let me stay in touch with the chubby, starry-eyed little kid who used to sing backup behind Connie on *Uncle Beano's Radio Hour.*

Mama had had a special publicity shot taken of us when we were on that show. I flipped through the scrapbook until I found it. There we were, two little girls in taffeta peasant outfits holding our tambourines high above our heads and smiling till our lips were welded to our upper teeth. I could still hear Mama coaching us through our big finale, which was a special arrangement of "The Italian Street Song" for two voices accompanied by a flute. In the middle of the cadenza we interpolated a chunk of the mad scene from *Lucia di Lammermoor.*

I closed the book, because I finally knew what was bothering me. There weren't going to be any actors on *Cee Gee!* I was still going to be in show business—sort of—but it wasn't the kind of show business I'd loved all my life. There wouldn't be anything to remind me of the Singing DaVito Sisters.

I knew what I had to do. I put on my coat, left the apartment, went down to the street, and hailed a cab.

Five minutes later when we pulled up in front of my old

studio, I told the cabbie to wait. I walked across the street and looked up at the big glitzy building I'd always thought was so pretentious.

"Goodbye," I said.

Then I got back in my cab and went home.

On the way back it started to snow—large flakes that were sticking. By morning the city would be blanketed in white. It would be like a clean slate, I told myself. It would be symbolic of my new beginning.

The next time I start thinking in terms of symbolism, I want someone to strangle me.

9

Cee Gee's studio was a symphony of mauves, grays, and maroons. A poster-sized blowup of Cee Gee with her trusty microphone hung on the wall behind the front desk. In honor of the season, the picture was festooned with pink-and-silver garlands which matched the huge silver and pink Christmas tree standing in the lobby. Under the tree were seven or eight shopping carts decorated with jazzy pink bows and crammed full of food. A pink wishing well stood nearby. On it was a sign reminding any visitor who felt like contributing to Cee Gee's Food Fund (For Our Less Fortunate Friends) that there were only two shopping days left until Christmas. I dropped in ten bucks and hoped against hope that the money would be used to buy something without fiber.

The lobby was spotless and silent—in my experience, an unnatural combo for a television studio. I walked up to the main desk and stated my business to a security team consisting of a male and female guard. After phoning someone somewhere in the building, the woman instructed me to follow the hallway to the elevator and take it to the second floor. She buzzed me through a locked glass door. I entered an immaculate corridor with flooring made out of a purple stone which does not occur in nature. More huge pictures of Cee Gee graced these walls. In each she was smiling and clutching a different trophy. For anyone whose memory needed a jog, the management had thoughtfully placed plaques nearby naming the awards for which these prizes had been given and the dates on which they were won. It was like being in a museum with extremely limited subject matter.

The elevator was ahead of me but I continued on past it— it couldn't hurt to scope out the place just a little, I figured. On the right side of the hallway were the hair and makeup rooms. On the left was a door which, according to the sign on it, led to the visitors' greenroom—a misnomer since the room was done in shades of plum. I knew because I checked it out. I was looking for people. By now, the lack of them had me spooked. I expect a television studio to be full of crazed humans running around screaming at each other as they try to do too much work in too little time and space. I expect temper tantrums, competitive cursing, and every once in a while, a food fight. I do not expect to hear my own footsteps echoing as I walk down fake marble halls. I started feeling the way I always do when I'm forced to visit the suburbs. After about three minutes I begin asking myself gloomy questions about the meaning of life. After five minutes I begin coming up with gloomy answers.

The hallway took a turn to the left as I reached the back of the building. On my right were double doors on which the word "Stage" was printed. Surely if there was any action in this mausoleum it would be in there. I opened the door and walked into a familiar blast of frigid air. So far so good. Sound-stages are always kept at subzero temperatures because that's the way the cameras like it and to hell with the humans, who aren't nearly as expensive. The room was dark, but I could see that it was set up like an auditorium with bleachers, a narrow stage, and a wide middle aisle.

When I looked it over, I finally realized why this floor of the building was so deserted. Because what was there for a technical crew to do on a talk show? Fifteen minutes before the show the minimum complement of stagehands allowed by the union would line up the guests' chairs on the stage and maybe set up Cee Gee's TelePrompTers if she used them. The cameras would be stationary, winging their shots on orders from the control booth. There were no booms because everyone would be individually miked. The hairdresser might brush a few strands out of a guest's face during the commercial break, or the makeup person might pat down an overly sweaty brow, but since this was a show about real people, only Cee Gee would be getting the full cosmetic treatment. There wouldn't be a wardrobe department in the way I knew and loved them; Cee Gee would have a personal stylist. It was all very depressing.

I was starting to leave when I heard sounds of life from the stage area at the back of the room. The lights went on and a calm voice started giving directions which I recognized as those of a lighting designer to his gaffer. Then the voice called out politely, "May I help you?"

I turned. The LD was a young man dressed in designer jeans and one of those artfully knitted sweaters with the seams on the outside. The kid's hair brushed his shoulders in a beautifully cut pageboy; a tasteful small gold hoop adorned one ear. His gaffer was only slightly less splendid. I wanted to inform them that they were a disgrace to their profession. Crew chiefs and their assistants were supposed to be harassed creatures who wore old work clothes, sweat, and smudges of grime. They did not, for Christ's sake, look like they had just stepped out of the pages of *GQ*. But at that moment the young man's face lit up with a friendly smile as he stepped closer.

"Angie?" he asked. "Angie DaVito? We heard you were coming on the show."

I looked more closely at him. There was something vaguely familiar about his face.

"I'm Joey Santucci. I'm Vinnie's kid," he said. Vinnie Santucci had been head of the stagehands crew on *Bright Tomorrow*. This elegant creature was Vinnie's son?

"Joey, my God. The last time I saw you, you were tripping over cables in my studio. Weren't you planning to be a forest ranger?"

"Yeah, well, you know how it is. Dad got me in the union and I figured what the hell . . ."

I gave him a big hug, grateful to know that some traditions remained intact in this new life of mine—like the nepotism in the technical unions, where a few families have been passing down their lucrative jobs from generation to generation for decades.

"You looking around, Angie?" Joey asked casually. A little too casually, it seemed to me. I could have sworn that he gave his buddy some kind of high sign. "You looking to see the control booth, maybe?"

"Hey, no fair planting the idea in her head," his colleague protested. "She's got to come up with it on her own."

"She is, dammit," said Joey. "All I did was ask a question. A couple of words."

"It was influencing the outcome—"

"Hold it." I came in over the top. "Joey Santucci, do you have a pool on me?"

When he grinned and flushed, I could see the resemblance to his dad.

"Well shit, Angie," he said sheepishly. "Things get awful dull in the staff lounge."

Staff lounge? They had a staff lounge? His father used to hang out on our loading dock with his crew. When he had time to hang out.

"You pissed?" he asked anxiously.

What I wanted to do was hug him again. Pools are another great tradition of the techies. They'll bet on anything from the possible wrap time after a tricky day's shooting, to the minute at which the vending machines will run out of diet Coke. Whenever my crew had run a pool on me I'd been flattered, seeing it as a sign that I belonged. And now this kid had one going on me before I'd even set foot in the building. At that moment I loved him deeply.

"Well, it is a hell of a welcome," I said sternly, for the benefit of his friend. But I was thinking hard. My territorial attitude toward my workplace was well known on my soap opera—also my nosiness. The bet had to be about how long it would take me to start investigating this joint.

"The fact is, I was planning to poke around for a second," I said. "Where's the control booth?"

"Through there," said Joey, indicating a door at the back of the studio. From the triumphant look on his face, I knew I'd been right. And that Joey had taken an early time in the pool.

Cee Gee's control booth was brand-new and well equipped, but much smaller than I'd thought it would be. I'd figured that it would go all the way to the end of the building, but clearly there was some other space on the back side of it. But what could it be? They wouldn't need a storage room because they didn't have any sets or props.

There was a door in the back wall. Telling myself I owed it to Joey to be thorough, I opened it.

Even in the dark I knew I'd walked into a second sound-stage. Although it was so small I couldn't imagine what it was used for. However, there was no mistaking the arctic temperature, the light grids in the gloom over my head, or the two cameras huddled together in front of me like large shadowy beasts.

And I was not alone. A heated conversation was in progress at the far end of the room.

I'm sure this world is full of folk who are so well evolved— or brain-dead—that the thought of hiding behind the cameras and shamelessly eavesdropping would not have occurred to them. Not me. Especially not when I heard my name mentioned.

". . . if Angela DaVito comes in here, there will be hell to pay," a flat, slightly nasal female voice was saying. "I'm warning you. You know what I can do—don't think I won't do it."

There was no response, just a beat of silence. Then the angry clip-clop of high heels on cement flooring told me that someone who was both heavy-footed and deeply angry was headed my way. I crouched lower behind my barricade. An amazon loomed up in the darkness. I couldn't make out particulars like facial features or hair color, but I did get a sense of size, shape, and an athlete's rolling gait. All suggested a woman who had at one time in her life played hearty sports involving shin pads—lacrosse, or possibly field hockey. She was wearing a dress that flowed—through the gloom I could make out a fussy flower print which was probably a mistake on one of her stature. I also caught a glimpse of pumps which would have been dainty in a smaller size.

For a moment I was afraid that her destination might be the control booth behind me, but she marched on to the opposite side of the studio.

She opened a door—a shaft of sunlight indicated that it was an exit to the outside. "Just remember what I can do," she called out before she slammed the door behind her.

Then there was silence. Whoever she had been talking to had not moved. The two of us were alone together in the dark. In the stillness I was sure I could hear myself breathe. Or maybe it was my unknown companion. Then, somewhere to my right, I heard a door open and close. Quietly this time. And very deliberately. I wondered if it was a trick—if whoever it was had seen me and was just pretending to leave the sound-stage. I started to shiver, and not just from the cold.

I told myself to stop being such a wimp. This was a function of my own overactive imagination. And the memory of a bad experience I'd had on the *Bright Tomorrow* soundstage during the murder investigation. But that was different. That time I'd been asking for trouble by playing detective. This wasn't the same thing at all. . . .

Somehow I found myself yanking at the control booth door. Then I was racing back through the main soundstage. I didn't stop running until I found Joey and his gaffer in the hallway. So call me a wimp.

10

"Why does this place have two soundstages?" I demanded from the boys as soon as I caught my breath.

The look on Joey's face as he turned to his buddy was one of pure delight. "See?" he said. "What did I tell you? Now write down the time."

"I still think you influenced the outcome," said his friend stubbornly.

"Why?" Joey was indignant. "Did I give her one clue? Did I say, 'Oh, by the way, there's a door at the back of the control booth,' or—"

"Gentlemen," I broke in loudly. "There is a question on the table."

"Sorry, Angie," said Joey. "That's where they keep the 'over my dead body' guests." He saw the look on my face. "Let me explain. Say you got these two sisters. Years ago they had a fight about something, who knows what . . ."

"Sex," offered his friend helpfully. "It's always about sex."

"Whatever. And these two sisters haven't talked to each other since forever. One of 'em wants to bury the hatchet, but the other doesn't. So the first one . . ."

"Call her Sister A," suggested his story consultant. "If you call them Sister A and Sister B, you can tell 'em apart."

Joey glared at his colleague before resuming his narrative.

"So the first sister will call or write to Cee Gee and tell her her story and that she'd like to talk to her sister again. And if the fight was full of human interest shit—or maybe it was about something that the production staff wants to do a panel on because of some hot new book somebody wrote—they'll bring in the two sisters. Only the one that won't talk may say she won't come on the show with the other. Like she'll say 'Over my dead body,' which is how we came up with the name for the second soundstage. So then they'll bring her on the show and tell her the other one isn't coming, but really the other one will be in the second soundstage watching the other one on the monitor."

He'd been unfair to his friend. Sister A and Sister B—or a scorecard—would have been real welcome. I was following him, but just barely.

"Then when the time is right, usually after the first commercial, Cee Gee will announce that the other one is here, and they'll punch up the cameras on her in the second soundstage and Cee Gee will start to interview her over the monitor about what the other one said."

"So they lie to the first sister," I said. "No, actually that would be the second one . . ."

"Sort of. But see, by then they're so mad that usually they want to get in each other's face, so Cee Gee brings 'em together during the commercial break and they scream and yell and—"

"Sometimes they spit at each other," interjected the gaffer. "Well, at least one lady did . . ."

"And then Cee Gee brings out the shrink, who tells them they have to feel each other's pain, and yada, yada, yada, and they'll start crying and Cee Gee will talk about the healing power of love and shit."

"But meanwhile the show has manipulated both of the women."

I don't know why it bothered me so much. Everyone knows that the talk shows use ambush tactics on their guests. But Cee Gee had always insisted in interviews that she was above that sort of thing. I guess because I was going to work for her I'd wanted to believe it. Joey smiled indulgently at my innocence.

"Angie, you gotta understand—this isn't like the soaps. We've got civilians here, not actors. These people don't know how to milk a moment. Sometimes when you're working with reality, you gotta organize it a little."

"Besides, people don't mind what you do to them as long as you put them on TV," offered the gaffer. "They'll say things to the whole world that I'd be ashamed to tell my priest if I was dying."

I gave up on the issue of ethics.

"How do they manage to keep the second guest hidden? Uh, I guess that would be Sister B."

"The second soundstage opens onto the street by a back exit. They sneak the guests in that way and keep them hidden in the soundstage until airtime. Cee Gee's dressing room opens onto the soundstage so she can go in and do the pre-interview before the show without anyone seeing her."

Interesting.

"So Cee Gee has access to the back soundstage," I said. "Are there any other entrances to it?"

"Only through the outside exit or the control booth," said Joey.

Which meant that my unknown companion in the sound-stage had ducked into Cee Gee's dressing room and might still be there.

"Where is Cee Gee's dressing room?"

"Over there. You want to see it?"

They led me to an unmarked door next to the main stage. Joey knocked, but there was no answer.

A chill ran through me as I remembered crouching in the darkness behind the cameras in the second soundstage.

"Uh, guys, this may not be such a good idea . . ." I began, but it was too late. Joey had already taken out his building passkey and unlocked the door.

It was a relief to find the room empty. And maybe just a bit of a letdown.

Cee Gee's dressing room was done in exactly the same style as her private quarters at home. Either she had a decorator with no imagination or an obsession with tufting that I didn't want to dwell on. The attached bathroom was also a repeat of her penthouse bathroom. Without the views. Or the fake blood. I spotted another door at the far end of the room.

"Is that the entrance to the second soundstage that you were talking about?" I asked Joey.

"Right. And she can also come from her office upstairs down here." He pointed to the back corner of the dressing room, where a small spiral staircase was partially hidden by a full-length mirror. "It's all one self-contained unit. Cee Gee can go from her office to tape the show and back without being seen by anyone."

Which meant that whoever had that quarrel on the second soundstage could have hightailed it back to the office via the dressing room with no one being the wiser. And since, according to Samantha, Cee Gee's office was never locked, that meant just about anyone in the building, theoretically. Also, by going through the soundstage it would be possible to get from the office to the street without being seen. So if someone—Grace Shipley for instance—wanted to steal something from Cee Gee's office—like a large doll—and sneak it out of the building, that's how she would do it. Very interesting.

11

We got back out in the hall just in time. A voice called out, "Whoohoo, Angie! There you are." Peggy Lawton hurried over to us. Joey rolled his eyes; his gaffer said hastily, "We better get back to work," and they vanished. Peggy did not seem to be a fave with the techies.

"I'm so glad I found you," she said cheerily, as we waited for the elevator. "It never occurred to me that you might get lost. This place is so simple."

"Well, you know how it is . . ." I gestured vaguely, and tried to change the subject. "They certainly do keep you interns busy."

She turned up the cheery knob another notch. "Oh, I'm not an intern," she said brightly. "Interns are college kids working for course credits. I can't afford college. But Townie has been letting me learn every aspect of the studio operation, and she said one day I might even become an associate producer. I go to production meetings and everything. It's just thrilling."

Cee Gee's plush elevator with the maroon suede wallpaper arrived and we got on. "Cee Gee and Townie have been so good to me," Peggy burbled on enthusiastically. "Cee Gee always says our show is one big happy family, and she's absolutely right. Everyone is just so kind."

When they're not threatening each other on darkened soundstages, or hanging their star in effigy, I thought.

"This is where the production offices are," my guide announced when we reached the second floor. It also seemed to be the heart of the operation. Thank God. I'd been hoping there was one somewhere. I looked around eagerly.

The ambience was still a bit cushy for my taste—everything was color-coordinated, including the arrangement of bare branches, pink and silver Christmas balls, and sprigs of ugly little pink orchids which sat on the main desk. But the energy on this floor was electric. Sitting behind the desk were three young women busily answering phones that rang nonstop. Behind them in the center of the floor was a rabbit warren of cubicles. People— mostly well dressed and female—called to each other over the partitions. They darted in and out of the offices that lined the outer walls, chattering and scuffing up the plush carpet. Everywhere I looked, piles of paper overflowed onto desks, chairs, and tables. Phones rang, fax machines clacked, copiers whirred, and computers hummed. There was a coffee stain on a mauve chair. Someone had left a half-eaten bagel on the arm of a couch.

This, I thought, was the way a studio should be.

Peggy led me to a large office at the back of the building with Hudson River views.

"Townie will be with you in just a moment. Can I get you some coffee or tea?"

"No thanks."

She left me to contemplate my surroundings.

I'd expected that Townie would favor the aggressively feminine decorating style that seems to be popular with powerful female television executives—and upscale hotel powder rooms. It's that brand of decor which features flowery chintzes, potpourri, and colors with food names like peach, cream, and mushroom.

But this room was a pleasant surprise. The chairs were covered in a practical corduroy. A white schedule board laying out the next two months of *Cee Gee!* tapings stretched over one wall. Next to it was a door which I assumed led to the adjoining office. Videotapes crammed the bookshelves. A chart posting the ratings of all daytime shows was hanging above them. Townie could tell at a glance if *Cee Gee!* was holding its own against the competition in both the weekly numbers and the overnights.

There was a photo of George on a large, shabby desk with a tooled leather top. Other than that, the only pictures in the room were hanging in a formal grouping on the right wall. They seemed to be framed publicity stills of an attractive woman, probably taken in the early part of the century. In most of them she was wearing what were obviously theatrical costumes, and striking melodramatic poses. Only one, which was larger then the rest, was a personal portrait. I had the feeling that I knew her—or that I'd seen pictures of her before—when I was a little girl, maybe at my Nana's house.

"Angie, welcome," said Townie. She'd come in from the other office. "I see you're looking at the gallery."

She was wearing a pearl-gray skirt which hit her about four inches above the ankle, a gray-and-white-striped vest, and a high-necked white blouse. It would have been the perfect ensemble to wear while marching for women's suffrage. Or while attending the Metropolitan Opera to hear the woman in the pictures sing *Madama Butterfly*.

"Geraldine Farrar!" I said. "Am I right?"

Her smile lit up her face.

"Yes indeed. She was my idol when I was a girl. I wanted to be the Farrar of my generation. How lovely that you were able to recognize her. Few people can."

"In my family she was right up there with Rosa Ponselle, Enrico Caruso, and the Pope. My grandparents tended to lump them all together. Although I'm not sure they would have stood in line for six hours to hear His Holiness sing '*Vesti la giubba.*'"

She laughed. "What a nice way to grow up. I knew you were the ideal person for us."

That wasn't quite the way I'd heard it from Samantha, but okay.

"Because I can recognize Geraldine Ferrar?"

"Because you have a sense of fun. I don't, I'm afraid. Neither do Felice and Cee Gee. I can be clever, and of course, Cee Gee has her smile, but we're really a rather humorless lot. It's our biggest weakness. Won't you sit down?"

I did. She slid gracefully into the chair behind her desk. "My biggest strength is that I'm methodical," she went on. "I've viewed tapes of your work on *Bright Tomorrow.* I like your attitude toward what you do. You don't try to stretch beyond the limits of your medium, yet you take it seriously."

I squirmed the way I always do when someone compliments me. I was about to say something humble, when she added, "I pride myself on having the same attitude." Which shut me up quite nicely.

Then her phone buzzed. She smiled a little apology at me and engaged in a brief conversation with someone about booking a show which I gathered would treat the burning issue of daughters who were embarrassed because their mothers were too fat. I tried hard not to overhear. Finally she hung up and turned back to me.

"As Cee Gee said last night, this is a turning point for us. We have our new facility and we've negotiated a deal with our distributor and one of the networks to do three original projects for them this year. Of course, *Cee Gee!* will remain the base of our strength, but if the new ventures are successful—and I have every intention of seeing to it that they are—that will be just the beginning. We're entering a new arena, Angie. And I'm certain that your background will be invaluable to us."

But according to Samantha, she'd had reservations about me.

"What kind of projects?" I asked.

"We're still discussing that. Personally, I see us working on theatrical material—movies of the week, possibly a pilot for a series."

"Do Felice and Cee Gee share your vision?"

And what was Grace's opinion before you fired her? I wondered but did not ask.

Townie turned away from me and looked off at the Hudson outside her window. A barge overflowing with garbage was floating by. On the top of the mound someone had planted a scraggly Christmas tree.

"Felice wants to be sure we don't stray from the kind of human interest material which has worked for us so far. As for Cee Gee . . ." She sighed. "Cee Gee has such a deep spirituality . . ."

I figured that translated to: "Felice wants to do more talk shows with folks named Bob, Earl, and Bambi, and Cee Gee favors inspirational specials featuring flavor-of-the-month gurus."

"It sounds as if there are some conflicts between you," I said.

"Have you ever known an organization of creative people in which everyone agreed all of the time?"

"No, but there does seem to be an unusual amount of tension on *Cee Gee!*"

"You mustn't judge us by what you saw the other night."

Actually, I'd been thinking about what I'd heard in the second soundstage. But I couldn't come up with a graceful way of mentioning it.

Townie stood up and headed for the door. "Come," she said. "There's something I want to show you."

We went back through the rabbit warren to the elevator. Her effect on the troops was interesting. No one actually stopped work to bob a curtsy as she passed, but you could feel that the impulse was there. And the motivating force behind it was not affection. That I got loud and clear.

"We're going to the third floor," said Townie as the elevator whisked us upward. "We just finished it this summer." I could feel her excitement. Then the door opened and we stepped out.

"Look," she said, her voice hushed with awe. And I understood why. Because the third floor took my breath away. First, there was the sheer size of it. "It was designed to be a completely flexible space," said Townie. "At the moment we produce all our own bumpers and promos up here, and we could probably shoot an entire feature film."

"You could rebuild the Baths of Caracalla and mount a production of *Aida* in this place," I said. She laughed happily.

"With this technology we have the capacity to broadcast a

live show anywhere in the world by satellite," she went on. "We can do simulcasts. Eventually we could get into interactive videos and a whole range of the new entertainment software. The possibilities are endless."

She showed me all of it. They had a state-of-the-art screening room, and editing facilities which were mind-boggling. Everywhere I looked, there were fancy new pieces of equipment I'd only heard about. But I knew I could work miracles with them. And oh, how I wanted to. For a brief moment all I desired in life was to use all this beautiful space and all these wonderful shiny new toys. I forgot about Townie standing beside me. I stood at the center of Cee Gee's new empire feeling a kind of heady power that was scary. Until a voice next to me brought me back to earth.

"It's mine," I heard Townie say softly. "I can do anything I want with it, and no one can stop me." I turned; her beautiful, aristocratic face was shining with the kind of rapture I usually associate with holy visions and places like Lourdes.

She turned to smile at me. "That tension you were talking about, Angie? All of that is ancient history now. We're putting the past behind us."

"Sometimes the past has a way of coming back."

"Not for us. This is our new beginning." She gestured to the gleaming expanse in front of us. "This will make it all worthwhile."

"Townie, come to your office, please." A frantic voice came over the PA system, breaking the mood. "Townie, it's May Day. Big-time."

She did an ironic little shrug. "Meanwhile, back to the bread and butter that pays the bills," she said.

———

When we got back down to her office, all hell had broken loose.

"Lyle is refusing to go on the show today," Peggy announced as we walked in. "He's back in his cell on the row crying, and the warden is trying to kick our camera crew off the prison grounds."

"Who's producing?"

"Jason. Lyle called him at his home last night to say he was getting cold feet, but they talked for an hour and a half and Jason thought he was okay."

"Jason knows that once they get cold feet, they're never okay. He should have gone upstate immediately to babysit Lyle until tape time."

"I think his wife gives him a hard time about taking off like that. She works too and—"

"Don't bore me with details, Peggy. Jason has not done his job." She looked at her phone. One of the buttons was lit. "Cee Gee's back in her office," she said. She picked up her phone and, to my surprise, punched the button, breaking into Cee Gee's conversation. "Cee Gee?" she said. "Sorry to interrupt, but we have an emergency. I'll be setting up a conference call for you in five minutes." She hung up and turned to Peggy. "Get on the phone with Lyle's girlfriend and offer her anything she wants if she'll put pressure on him. Just make sure what we pay her is less than what we're paying him. Then call Legal and tell them that I want to terminate Jason's contract. We don't tolerate sloppy work on *Cee Gee!*"

I thought of the pictures of the staff in *Family Circle* and wondered which one was the hapless Jason. I wondered if Legal would be efficient enough to hand him his walking papers by Christmas, or if they'd come as a New Year's present.

Townie turned to me. "Angie, I'm afraid we're going to

have to cut this short," she said. She got up from behind her desk and walked me to the door. Behind us Peggy began making frantic phone calls. But Townie was strolling as if she had all the time in the world.

"Why don't you come back to the studio next week?" she suggested. "We won't be taping again until after New Year's, but we do have production meetings. You can have the rest of the studio tour and see how we operate. Unless you'll be out of town for that week?"

"No. I go to my sister's house in Connecticut for Christmas, but I'm always back in a couple of days." Or sooner if I can swing it.

"Perfect. Where is your sister's place?" She continued her unhurried pace as we retraced our steps to the elevator.

"New Milford."

"How lovely. George and I pass by New Milford on our way to our country place. We bought a house about two miles away from Cee Gee's farm. It's beautiful country."

If you like the country. Personally, I feel if you've seen one tree you've seen them all.

"Our place isn't nearly as grand as Cee Gee's. It's just a little getaway. We don't even keep any staff out there, which George loves. We'll go out tomorrow for the holiday. Of course, we'll be spending Christmas Day with Cee Gee."

Of course. Didn't they ever get sick of seeing each other?

"I'll talk to Felice. Maybe we can all get together."

"Mmmmn," I said, hoping it would pass for an answer. Privately, I promised myself that whatever else might happen to me on Christmas, I would not spend any part of it with Cee Gee and the gang.

It was another one of those moments when a premonition or two wouldn't have hurt.

———

When I got outside, just for the fun of it I made a fast detour around the building. I have a pretty good sense for space and floor plan layouts—it's probably a result of all those years of fitting four full sets plus limbo areas into one soundstage when I was producing *Bright Tomorrow*—and sure enough, there was the back entrance, right where I thought it would be. It was a small steel door marked "Warning, Emergency Exit Only." But Joey was right—it could also be used as an entrance by anyone who had a key to the lockbox in the upper right-hand corner.

Satisfying my curiosity about the back entrance made me feel a little more on top of things somehow—I'm not sure my need to know is always a positive character trait.

12

Christmas never depressed me until Connie got married. I enjoyed the way we celebrated the holiday when I was a kid. That's because Connie and I were usually on a stage performing. There was always some organization somewhere that wanted to see us play Christmas dolls who came to life, and hear our medley of "White Christmas," "Ave Maria," "The Italian Street Song," and the chunk of Lucia's mad scene.

But then Connie got away from Mama and show business and settled down to domestic bliss with Arnie, who is sweet and who loves her, which is the good news. He is also a very successful accountant, which is not so good, because my sister does not have to work outside the home and has chosen instead to focus her formidable energies on being, in her own words, "a creative wife and mommy." The operative word being "creative." Especially at Christmas.

Usually I find reasons to stay in the city as long as I can on Christmas Eve Day. That way I don't have to help assemble the Early American gingerbread house. Or help set up the Victorian skating scene. Or help make the spun sugar angels for the top of the Lane cake—a confection which was created by a sadist in the early eighteenth century who began the recipe with the words "Choppe ye raisins into perfecte thirds."

———

So, on the morning of the twenty-fourth, I rose late, and took as long as I dared to get on my way. I washed out my hand laundry, and gave myself a pedicure. I spent at least fifteen minutes rearranging the ornaments I hang on my snake plant each Christmas. Why buy a tree if you're going to be out of town?

Finally, it was twelve-thirty and I knew I'd dawdled as long as I could. It was time to face the music. And the two-hour bus trip into northwestern Connecticut. With all the other merry holiday travelers. And their large awkward bundles. And their small active children.

I caught the one o'clock Greyhound local out of Port Authority. My seatmate was a teenager of indeterminate sex who did not seem to have bathed recently. In front of me sat five-year-old Tiffany, who was traveling with Mommy and her brother Alexander. Lexy, she confided, suffered from motion sickness. Especially in vehicles that did a lot of starting and stopping. She mentioned this fact as the bus began jerking its way down Ninth Avenue. I told myself sternly that I was going to be cheerful; the bus ride would only last for two hours.

Thanks to a propane gas truck which had jackknifed across the highway somewhere north of Danbury, the ride took three hours, forty-two minutes, and eighteen seconds. Lexy threw up twice.

Arnie and the family dog, Ralphie, were listlessly waiting for me in front of the New Milford bus station. Normally both are ebullient creatures—especially Ralphie, who is young, large, vigorous, of vague parentage, and not exactly the Einstein of the canine set. But even Ralphie was bright enough to know when he was making an ass of himself. Which he was at that moment in his red cross-stitched Christmas coat with *Ho, Ho, Ho* embroidered on it. And his red ear bows.

"Hey Ralphie. Give me the paw?" I asked. It was our standard greeting. He shot me a baleful look and hung his head.

"I don't think he's very happy with his ensemble, Arnie," I said.

"Yes," said Arnie, who was wearing a red sweatsuit on which large fabric decals of Santa had been glued and outlined in green fabric paint. "Merry Christmas," he added glumly. And led me to his station wagon.

"I'm sorry I'm so late," I said. "Did I miss much?"

"Just the Lane cake."

"Oh gee. Well, it really wasn't my fault. There was a terrible accident. I understand traffic has been tied up for hours . . ."

"You always miss the Lane cake, Angie," Arnie said darkly. Then he added, "Quit it, Ralphie." The dog was launching a sneak attack on the back end of his holiday coat. He yelped in surprise when he bit his own tail instead. "You can't get out of that thing," said Arnie. "So quit trying."

We shoved Ralphie into the back seat of the car and headed toward the split level Tudor Arnie and Connie and their two kids call home.

"Fuck Martha Stewart," said Arnie, who never swears.

I sighed. The weekend stretching out ahead of me was going to be endless. I would have killed for a reason to go back to the city.

As it turned out, that would not be necessary.

13

"Aunt Angie, you had a phone call," said Arnie junior after we'd done the Christmas greetings and Connie had laid her Christmas guilt trip on me for being late. "They didn't say who it was, but Maria Lucia has the number."

The phone picked up after the first ring, but no one answered. "Hello?" I said.

"Is this Angela DaVito?" whispered a voice I could barely recognize.

"Yes. Is that you, Sa—"

"Don't," said Samantha quickly. "Don't say my name out loud if there are people there."

"All right, Sa—Susie. What's wrong?"

"Could you come to the apartment, Angie? Right away?"

"Honey, I'm in Connecticut."

"Please, Angie."

"Sa—Susie, it's Christmas Eve."

"Please."

"Are you alone?"

"I'm supposed to be in the country with Felice. Just come fast, Angie." And she hung up.

"But you can't go back to New York," Connie wailed.

"Just for tonight. I'll be back out on the first bus tomorrow morning."

"You'll miss all the fun. We've been waiting until you got here to bake the icicle cookies."

The woman has known me all my life and she still doesn't realize that I'd rather crawl over hot coals than bake cookies.

"Your cookies are the best ones, Aunt Angie," chimed in my niece, Maria Lucia, who at ten is already giving her mother a run for her money. "They always look like penises."

During the mother-daughter conflict which followed this statement I managed to make my escape.

"Look, Arnie, I wouldn't do this if my friend Susie weren't in real trouble," I said as he drove me back to the bus station in sullen silence. "It's her first Christmas since Jack left her for that little figure skater." When you work in daytime drama you develop a flair for story telling. "She was talking about taking pills. I only hope I'm in time," I added with what I thought was a nice touch.

"I hate you, Angela," said Arnie.

Naturally, since I had the bus almost completely to myself, the mess on the highway had been cleared up and we made the trip back to Manhattan in record time. There wasn't even a small traffic jam to impede our progress. It made me feel even guiltier than I already had been feeling.

When I got back to New York I knocked down two people while running through the bus terminal, grabbed the last cab on the line, effectively blocking a guy with skis and muscles, and spent the entire ride to Cee Gee's apartment leaning forward and screaming, "Faster!" into the cabbie's ear. Given the prevailing holiday mood in the city, it was a miracle that no one pulled a weapon on me.

Samantha had had the presence of mind to alert the doorman; he let me in the building the minute I said my name. When I rang the buzzer upstairs the door opened immediately, as if someone had been waiting for me.

"Angie?" said Townie. She looked stunned. Behind her stood Felice, looking equally bewildered.

"What the hell are you doing here?" Felice asked.

14

"I called her," said Samantha. All three of us turned to see Cee Gee and Sam standing at the top of the stairs. Cee Gee looked a little wobbly. Samantha's arm was around her.

"You did what?" shrilled Felice, and started for the staircase, but Townie stopped her.

"Samantha may be right," she said. "Angie might know what to do. She has been through this before."

"Yeah, come upstairs, Angie," said Cee Gee. Her crisp, TV-trained speech was slurred and she was holding what looked like an industrial-strength drink. Felice had one too. Townie did not.

"I thought you wanted to wait for George before we did anything," Felice said to Townie.

"I do. Angie, if you please?"

So we made our way up the swirling white staircase in silence. And walked silently along the white hallway to Cee Gee's white bedroom. Then at the door, Cee Gee suddenly lurched and announced, "I'm going to puke."

"Not in your bathroom." Townie's voice was pitched just a little too high.

"We'll go to Samantha's," said Felice, and eased her off in the opposite direction.

Which meant it was Samantha, Townie, and I who went

into Cee Gee's white-on-white bathroom. The Cee Gee doll was sitting on the hamper the way I'd left her. And there was no fake blood on the walls. But for some reason I couldn't explain, I didn't want to see what was on the floor. I didn't look until Sammy said, "Angie?" in a shaky whisper. So I looked down. Which is when I saw the thin trickle of real blood oozing out of the gunshot wound in a very dead body.

15

As I stared at the female form splayed out on Cee Gee's monogrammed bathmat, I felt something cold work its way up the back of my neck. I knew that body. Or, to be more precise, I knew the shape of it. And there was no way to mistake those D-width feet crammed into the flimsy pumps with the gold buckles on the vamps. This was the person who had been talking about me in the second soundstage at Cee Gee's studio. I was willing to bet I knew her name.

"It's Grace," said Townie quietly.

Bingo, I thought.

I turned to look at Townie. Her eyes were large and dark, as if the pupils had dilated to fill the irises. But that was the only hint of the incredible strain she had to be under. Sammy stood next to her, equally stolid. It occurred to me that in some ways they were two of a kind. I wondered which one of them would dislike the thought more. For some reason, the idea made me want to giggle.

"Angie? You okay?" asked Samantha. I forced myself to take a deep breath. I put on what I hoped was not a sick smile. I was not going to fall apart in front of these people. Especially since everyone knew this was not my first experience with this kind of thing. When the dead body turned up in the *Bright Tomorrow* studio—on the makeup table in the star dressing room, but that's another story—I was one of the unlucky few who saw it. Unfortunately, the incident didn't seem to have steeled me for this one.

"I think I'd better go somewhere else," I said. I concentrated on walking steadily into the bedroom, where I sat on Cee Gee's chaise longue. Then I gasped as something soft and fuzzy brushed against my arm. I looked down to see an outsized politically incorrect mink coat humped up beside me. Next to it was a purse. The clasp was a repeat of the gold buckle that decorated the shoes on the body in the bathroom. And I'd thought matching purses and shoes went out in the early sixties with beehive hairdos. Live and learn.

"Does that belong to . . . ?" I began.

"Yes, it's Grace's," said Townie. "Perhaps it would be best if we went downstairs now." Samantha and I followed her out of the bedroom.

When we reached the top of the stairs, the doorbell rang.

"It's probably the police," I said.

But it was George, calling through the door, "Vicky? Are you there?"

I will always admire people who can do the stiff-upper-lip thing. Probably because there is no way in hell I ever could. If I had been Townie, I'd have raced downstairs and thrown myself into my husband's arms, sobbing hysterically. Or maybe I'd have burst into uncontrollable laughter. What I wouldn't have done was open the door calmly and say with only the slightest of quivers, "George, thank goodness."

George, however, was more demonstrative. He took her in his arms and stroked her hair with a look of such tenderness that I felt funny about watching. Samantha was made of sterner stuff.

"Grace . . . The body is upstairs in Mama's bathroom," she said. "George, if you want to come up . . ."

At that Townie pulled herself out of his embrace. "No," she said.

"I don't mind, darling," he said.

"There's no need."

"Whatever you say, Vicky." He looked up to the landing where Samantha and I were still standing. "Samantha, I thought you and Felice were supposed to be in the country. And why is Angie here?"

"Samantha called me."

He smiled at Sammy. "How very clever of her."

"I'm going into the kitchen," said Townie. "Cee Gee will be ready for some tea and I could use a cup myself." And such was the power of her personality that the rest of us followed her without a murmur.

The kitchen was a big room, very white, and full of stainless-steel equipment. My mind flashed unpleasantly to thoughts of morgues and autopsy tables. I told myself I'd have to stop watching those old *Quincy* reruns.

Townie began making tea with an efficiency that surprised me. I'd pegged her as the type who wouldn't know what a kettle was.

"We have to decide how to handle this, Angie," she said.

"There's not much you can do until the police get here," I said.

"Oh, we haven't called them yet," said Samantha grimly.

"You what?"

"Townie wanted to wait until we'd had a chance to come up with the right story for the press."

"You're kidding." I turned to Townie, who was measuring tea leaves and putting them into a silver strainer. "Don't you watch cop shows on television? It's probably a felony—or worse— not to report a murder for . . . how long has it been since you found the body?"

"Too long," she said. "And I fully understand that. But at this point, a few minutes more won't hurt. And we have to have a game plan."

"Jesus," said Samantha.

For the first time Townie came close to losing it. She whirled on Samantha and snapped, "I'll thank you to keep a civil tongue in your head!"

"Don't you realize how this looks? Grace is dead in Mama's apartment. Everyone knows how Mama and Grace felt about each other. Now you're holding off on going to the police. You're making Mama look guilty, Townie."

"I'm doing nothing of the sort. Besides, your mother can account for every moment of her time today."

"I don't give a shit. You've got to stop fucking around. This is serious."

"How dare you tell me what to do? I'm the one who's taken care of Cee Gee all these years. I cleaned up the messes, I handled the problems—"

"Well, you're not handling this one. And if you don't call the fucking cops, I will."

Townie drew back her hand in the classic position to deliver a slap, but George moved in quickly.

"Vocabulary aside, Samantha is right, darling."

"I have to keep the press out of it until we're ready for them, George. You know that. I have to handle this delicately."

"Look at me, Vicky. You can't control this."

"Yes I can. I've done it before. Felice will work with the PR people. There are ways to present things so that—"

"Not this time. This time you are just going to have to let whatever happens happen."

"I can't."

"Of course you can, Townie," said Cee Gee from the doorway. We all turned. She wasn't completely steady on her feet, but she didn't look too much the worse for wear. Obviously her recuperative powers were amazing. "We're going to call the police and let them discover the truth as soon as possible. Angie, don't you have friends on the force?"

"There is one detective I know slightly."

"Would you call him?"

"Cee Gee, the fans . . ." Townie began.

"The fans will have nothing but sympathy for us."

"But . . ."

"I know my audience, Townie." Then she walked over to her and put an arm around her. "Don't worry," she said. "It's all going to be all right. It's not as though we have anything to hide."

Given my experiences with the group, that had to be one of the funnier statements I'd heard, but no one laughed.

Finally Townie asked, "Angie, would you call your friend, please?"

So I called Teresa O'Hanlon.

16

Detective Teresa O'Hanlon and I were not close buddies. We met when she was assigned to investigate the *Bright Tomorrow* murder, and I suppose you could say that we'd worked together, although I'm not sure it would thrill her to hear it phrased that way. We hadn't kept in touch since. However, I had gotten to know a little about her through the course of "our" case.

Teresa is a third-generation cop who proudly carries the shield her father and grandfather wore before her. She plays strictly by the rules. Until she feels the rules aren't working for the good guys. In which case she will bend them with remarkable abandon. I liked her for that. I think she liked me in spite of herself.

I was a little surprised to find her working on Christmas Eve when I called; it seemed to me that kind of duty would be shunted off on lesser members of the department.

"I've volunteered to work this shift for the past few years," she explained when I expressed my surprise. "It keeps someone with kids from having to do it." Teresa is childless and a widow; the late Bobby O'Hanlon was a narcotics officer shot in the line of duty. To me the word "widow" connotes gray hair under a tasteful hat, so I find it hard to apply it to someone who is in her mid-thirties and has a mane of red hair, perfect skin, and a figure a professional actress would die for. What's depressing about all of this is that Teresa's the kind of woman other women know has never spent two minutes obsessing on her inner thighs or using an alpha hydroxy moisturizer.

"So what's *your* excuse for working on the holiday, Angie?" she asked.

It was the first time it had occurred to me that that was what I was doing.

"I need your help. Actually, it's a friend of mine—well, more of an acquaintance. Acquaintances, actually . . ."

"Angie, what's wrong?"

"I . . . They want to report a murder."

There was a long silence on the other end of the phone. I pictured Teresa closing her eyes. When she spoke again, she sounded very, very calm. "Suppose you tell me exactly what you've gotten yourself into," she said. As I drew breath to start, she added pleasantly, "And Angie? Don't leave anything out."

Since Townie, Felice, and Cee Gee were standing within hearing distance, that was not going to be possible. There was no way I could fill her in on my little eavesdropping escapade in the second soundstage—among other things. But I did give her the basics.

When I finished, Teresa sighed. "Why do I have the feeling I've been here before?"

"How do you think I feel?" I demanded. "You're used to seeing dead bodies. It's your job."

"What do you want me to do for you, Angie?"

"I told these people you're the one to handle this case."

There was a pause. When she spoke again, if I hadn't known it was Teresa I'd have thought she sounded hesitant. "Why me?"

"I trust you. There's a lot at stake."

"There usually is in a murder."

"Can you take it on?"

Again that funny little hesitation.

"There are some layers of command."

"This bunch can cut through them."

"What about you?"

"Me? What do you mean?"

"Are you planning to stay out of this one? I'm just curious."

"I did not interfere with your investigation the last time."

"I could have brought you in on obstruction charges on four separate occasions."

"Well, this is different. I never even met the woman who was killed."

Surely a near miss in a darkened soundstage didn't count.

"You're saying you're not involved emotionally with these folks?"

"Exactly."

"Which is why you came in from Connecticut on Christmas Eve to help them. All right, Angie, we're on our way." And she hung up.

Teresa was right, of course. I was emotionally involved. With one member of the group anyway—the youngest. And I was afraid she might be in trouble. So that was why I let the others stay huddled together in the kitchen, sipping Townie's tea and waiting for the constabulary, while I pulled Samantha aside into the dining room.

"We haven't much time," I said. "Teresa and her squad will be here any minute. Now tell me fast—what was going on between you and Grace Shipley?"

She gave me her toughest deadpan. "I don't know what

the fuck you're talking about," she said. But her face went from rosy pink to a shade of tomato red.

"Sammy, I've dealt with kids your age who act for a living, so no way can you bullshit me. Besides, you've got the wrong skin tone for lying. Talk."

She thought it over for a beat; then she took a deep breath. "I'm the reason Grace was fired. It's all my fault."

"Tell me about it."

"There was this guy on the show, he did the audience warm-up . . ."

"David?"

"No. Although David's another one."

"Another what?"

"Shitheel. What is it about comedians? Why are they all such sons of bitches?"

"Early narcissistic trauma. Bad potty training. Who knows? Go on with your story."

"This guy did warm-up before David. His name was Robert Morton. And he was getting it on with Grace."

"An intern? But Grace must have been in her late thirties or early forties . . ."

"She was old enough to have been his goddamn grandmother. Although Robert wasn't an intern—or a kid. He moved over from the PR division. Grace gave him the slot after the two of them . . ."

"Became an item?"

"He was fucking her brains out, Angie. Robert has a lot of talent in that department."

A light was beginning to dawn.

"And you know this because . . ."

"Because then Robert and I . . ."

"Became an item."

"I know it was a stupid thing to do, but he's a real stud muffin, you know? Besides, he was the one who hit on me. He told me it was a sexual harassment thing with Grace—he had to do her to keep his job. I guess I knew he was lying about that. I mean, I knew that he was using her, but . . . I kidded myself about him. You know how sometimes when a guy is real hunky you do that? Tell yourself everything's cool with him when you know it isn't?"

I knew.

"And of course he was just using me, too," she said quietly. "To get to Mama." For a moment she was lost in thought. I wondered how many other people in her young life had used her to get to Mama.

"The shit really hit the fan when Grace found us. She was crazy to get back at me. Sounds like an episode from Mama's show, doesn't it?"

That had been my thought exactly.

"So what did Grace do to you?"

For some reason this seemed to make her clam up again. "Just stuff," she mumbled.

"Such as?"

No answer. Her face returned to its earlier tomato hue. Behind us there was a knock at the door, and Townie opened it to the cops in uniform. As I recalled it, they were the ones who showed up first at a murder scene. Teresa wouldn't be far behind them.

"Samantha, we don't have time to play games. Now, a couple of days ago when I was watching your mother's show, I saw something. A man asked a question about you—"

"Shit, did that thing air already?"

One of the cops was talking to Townie; another was holding an ardent conversation with his walkie-talkie—or whatever the hell you call those things cops talk into that seem to produce so much static.

"So you knew about the slipup?"

"That was no slipup. Grace let it stay in deliberately. By the time Townie realized what she'd done, it was too late to get the tape back from the affiliates."

"What was the man talking about?"

No answer. But she was embarrassed. I couldn't imagine what might embarrass Samantha Jones.

"Sammy, come on. The clock is ticking."

"All right. Shit. It happened when I was just a kid, okay? One summer I got caught shoplifting from a drugstore up in Connecticut. It was no big deal. I mean it was, because I shouldn't have been stealing, but I was just eleven years old and Townie wasn't letting me wear makeup because she's always been afraid about Mama's image because I'm a bastard, and it wasn't fair because then they sent me to this school where all the girls were these rich bitches who had been wearing lipstick and eye shadow for years. So one day I took some. I mean it's not like I was headed for a life of fucking crime or anything. But that's the way Grace made it sound when she told it to the tabloids."

"And that was when your mother fired Grace."

"Not exactly. Mama wanted to do it then, but Townie wouldn't. Then Grace did the shit with that show you saw, and Mama went ape. She fired Grace's ass so fast Townie couldn't do anything. Afterward, Townie kept trying to make Mama change her mind—but nothing doing. Grace was history."

"So how long has it been since your mother fired Grace?"

"Maybe six weeks. That's the usual lag time between when they tape a show and when it airs."

It figured. It had been about six weeks since Freddie first heard the rumors that Cee Gee Jones was looking for a new senior producer. And from the sound of it, Townie had spent most of that time arguing to reinstate Grace.

"Sammy, why was Townie so determined to keep Grace with the show?"

"Who knows?"

But she waited a beat too long before she said it. She wasn't lying, but she was holding something back. I knew it. Meanwhile the cops had concluded their business with Townie, and everyone was heading upstairs. The walkie-talkie was still making a racket.

"Was there any other reason?"

"No."

But again it came a little too slow. I tried a shift in gears.

"What were you doing in New York today?"

"I live here."

"Very funny. You said on the phone you were supposed to be in the country with Felice. So what happened?"

"Felice and I both stayed in town last night. At her apartment. Nobody knew."

"What about the servants at the house in Connecticut?"

"It's just the cook and the housekeeper who are out there full-time. Felice paid them off the way she always does."

"She does this a lot?"

Samantha shrugged uncomfortably. "I didn't mean that." The cops had disappeared from the upstairs landing; presumably they'd gone into Cee Gee's bedroom.

"What did you do in the city today?"

"I had to see someone."

"Who?"

Pause.

"Samantha . . ."

"Robert. But it wasn't what you think. He called me and he said he was going to one of those gonzo news shows with the whole story about Grace and me. I was trying to stop him."

So he might be her alibi. If she needed one. I could feel my stomach muscles tighten at the thought.

"Where is Robert now?"

"Probably flying out to L.A. in first class with the money I gave him. The prick thinks he's going to be the next Tim Allen." She shook her head in disbelief. "How I could ever have—"

"Where did you get the money?"

"Felice. I mean, I guess it was Mama's money really, but Felice gave it to me. Felice can always get her hands on money when she needs it."

"Why didn't Felice go see Robert herself?"

"She was busy."

"Doing what?"

"I don't know. I'm not fucking with you, Angie. All I know is, sometimes she takes off and she never tells anyone about it."

If she did know more, I didn't have time to pry it out of her. The cops had come back out onto the upstairs landing. I had one more question. The one I didn't want to ask.

"Sammy, how angry were you at Grace?"

It took her a second, but when she finally got it, she did a double take that would have been funny if she hadn't been so outraged.

"You mean was I pissed enough at her to off her in my mother's bathroom? Just take a gun and . . . Jesus, Angie, what do you think I am?"

The anger was mixed with a hurt which was so real I knew

she couldn't have faked it. Sammy wasn't leveling with me about something—but whatever it was, I was sure she hadn't committed the murder. Not that I'd really thought she might have . . . Still, I felt my stomach muscles relax. Then over Samantha's shoulder I saw Teresa enter the foyer. "Sammy, I know you're hiding something," I hissed. "I want to know what it is."

"I can't—"

"Oh yes you can tell me. And you will. But not now. For now, just remember that Detective O'Hanlon is very smart, and you're not a kid as far as these people are concerned. You're old enough to have had an affair with the man who was sleeping with Grace."

"But—"

"Call me, Sammy, I want the whole story." I walked away. But not fast enough. Teresa had spotted us.

"Good evening, Angie," she said. "Discussing the case already?"

"That's Samantha Jones—Cee Gee Jones's daughter. I was trying to comfort her. Naturally, she's terribly upset by what has happened."

"Naturally. And I'm sure you'll tell me everything she said when you and I have our little talk later."

She moved off to join her second in command, a black detective named Hank, whom I knew by sight from my last encounter with our city's finest. They were joined by a detective I didn't remember. Which wasn't significant, since I didn't exactly hang out with the police. What was significant was the feeling I had that Hank and Teresa were not fond of their coworker, who was in his fifties, wore plaid polyester, and should have been more diligent about doing his daily sit-ups. Teresa was maintaining an air of bland professionalism. Hank, who had a fabulous set of dimples when he smiled, was too glum to display them.

But when the crime-scene unit arrived it was clear that everyone was in a bad mood. From the snatches of muttered conversation I overheard, I gathered that the photographer was risking divorce if she didn't get home in time to watch her husband play Santa for the twins. Another officer had spent the entire trip in from Suffolk County on the car phone trying to guide his wife through the intricacies of assembling a toy stove.

The arrival of Cee Gee's lawyer didn't do much to lighten everybody's mood.

"We may be able to contain the situation for a few hours," he drawled in patrician tones. "Thank God it's Christmas Eve." It was not a sentiment designed to thrill the disgruntled police. Nor did it help that he was wearing a velvet smoking jacket and an ascot.

After some negotiation, Teresa and the lawyer agreed that the second floor would be a good spot for questioning Cee Gee and company. As we began trooping upstairs, Teresa detached me from the rest of the crowd. "I think it might be better if you weren't hanging around here getting into trouble, Angie," she said. "I'll have Hank drive you over to the precinct. You can wait for me in my office."

"The precinct? Why can't you question me here?"

"Because I want you out of my hair."

"I'll sit quietly by myself. I won't talk to anyone. I'll read a magazine."

"You can bring the magazine to the police station. Wait here while I get Hank . . ."

"Never mind. I'll go by myself."

She looked at me dubiously.

"Teresa, what am I going to do? Skip out of town? For what reason?"

"I don't know. That's what bothers me . . ." She looked at me some more. Finally she said, "All right, I'll see you in my office. And then you can tell whatever it was you didn't tell me during our phone call."

Like me, Teresa has a special radar for the half-truth. I slunk off to get my coat.

17

It had gotten colder while I was in Cee Gee's apartment. And the city seemed to have emptied out. The frigid wind whipped up and down a deserted Park Avenue.

The good part was that there was no press gathered outside Cee Gee's building. Yet. They would arrive eventually, but for the moment, score one for the discretion of the co-op staff in a time of paid tabloid informers.

The bad part was that the ancient doorman ignored my hints about getting me a taxi. He was too busy glaring at the small fleet of cop cars double-parked at his curb. So I headed out into the night on my own.

There wasn't a cab in sight. However, other official-looking vehicles were barreling toward the building. It was time to be elsewhere. I started walking.

After four hand-and-feet-numbing blocks I spotted a lone taxi on the opposite side of the street. Screaming, "Cabbie, wait!" I sprinted for it.

I don't know why I didn't see the bucket of white poinsettias. It was part of the floral display set up in the median which runs through the center of Park Avenue. Maybe I missed it because I was so focused on nabbing what seemed to be the last taxi on earth. Maybe I was off balance because my feet had turned to blocks of ice. Whatever. I tripped over the damn flowers. Which caused me to do an interesting ballet across the remaining half of the avenue. The cab stopped at the precise moment I hit the pavement, knees first. In great pain.

"You are drunking too much?" asked the driver anxiously, as I dragged myself into his vehicle. "Not get sick in my cab?"

"I fell down," I said with forced calm, "because someone has turned Park Avenue into an obstacle course."

"Better you get out of cab," said the driver. "You get sick, boss make me clean up." He folded his arms to indicate that he was unwilling to move, and turned on his radio.

"The only way you will get me out of this car is to throw me out bodily," I shouted over the din of a rock station. "And trust me, that is something you do not want to try. I have been a single woman living in Manhattan for many years. Now take me to the Twentieth Precinct station house. It's in the Eighties between Columbus and Amsterdam. I can't give you an exact address but I'll know the street when I see it."

The cabbie wasn't budging. "American women," he snorted in disgust. "In my country a woman does not have liberation. Much better. No Madonna. No drunk," he added pointedly.

I'd ripped my panty hose, and cut the palms of both hands. One knee was bleeding rather freely. The other was starting to throb. I leaned forward and gave him a drunken leer. "You'd better get a move on," I slurred. "I'm not feeling so good."

As we raced off into the night, some rock star on the radio began butchering "O Little Town of Bethlehem."

By the time we reached the police station I was wearing a king-sized chip on my shoulder. It was Christmas Eve and I was spending my holiday with dead bodies and the police. Added to which, I hurt. And it might be hours before I could go home and have the hot bath I craved. The cheery thought that I'd brought all my woes on myself by ducking out on the family fun in Connecticut did nothing to improve my disposition.

Getting out of the cab proved to be a challenge. My right knee had stopped bleeding and started to swell. The left knee had gone from throbbing to drum riffs. I had to use both lacerated hands to open the car door. As I hobbled up the steps to the front door of the police station, I muttered freely to myself.

At that moment a car raced up to the curb and screeched to a halt. I don't know much about cars except that I drive them badly and as infrequently as I can manage. But even I could tell that the vehicle which had pulled up in the no-parking zone in front of the police station was something special.

It was low-slung, in a shade of gray somewhere between silver and steel. From front to back it screamed good design, elegance, and big bucks.

A man in a Gianni Versace coat emerged from the driver's side and raced past me, nearly knocking me down.

"Excuse me," I yelled, giving him the New Yorker's time-honored battle cry against random rudeness. It's the spin you put on the "scuse" that lets the other guy know you mean business.

This bozo didn't even slow down long enough to snarl, "Whyn't you watch where you're going?" Which is the standard— though not by any means the only acceptable—reply. He slammed the door in my face.

"Go back to New Jersey," I shouted after him. Not one of

my better insults, but then, I wasn't at my best. Besides, he couldn't hear me.

It took me a couple of minutes to reopen the door and make my painful way to the front desk. By that time the whirl-wind in the coat had vanished into the bowels of the building.

I'd visited this police station before. It hadn't been what I'd call a cheery place, but it had been lively. On Christmas Eve it was empty and bleak. There wasn't a gray head in sight—obviously, anyone with seniority and clout was spending the evening at home with the family. Someone had tried to intro-duce a festive note into the station with a plastic menorah, a fake Christmas tree, and a red sign that said "Happy Holidays." The attempt had been a mistake.

I shuffled up to the desk sergeant, who was expecting me, Teresa the Efficient having alerted him. Since her office was on the second floor, he waved me through to the elevators. Three cops huddled around a small, desk-size TV watching Jimmy Stewart in *It's a Wonderful Life*. I limped ostentatiously as I made my way to the elevator, but no one seemed to care. I wondered what level of injury would make this hardened group take notice. Then I thought again and decided that ig-norance was probably bliss on that one.

Since I'd been to Teresa's office on my previous visits, I knew where to find it. Actually, to dignify her small cubicle with the word "office" was stretching a point. It was a corner of the main room which had been enclosed with drywall and windows on two sides. The result was a tiny space, made smaller by the parade-size American flag which dominated one half of it.

As I came closer to the office, I saw through the window

that there was someone inside. Someone who had taken off his Versace coat to reveal that he was wearing the latest fashion in men's slacks. Possibly from Dolce & Gabbana. Or maybe it was Dries Van Newton.

You get to know the names—and price tags—of trendy menswear when you spend years of your life producing a soap opera. Outfitting male sex symbols is, after all, a significant part of the job.

The man, who was facing away from me, was writing something on Teresa's desk. Which meant he was bending over slightly.

I opened the door in my new two-fisted style. "Hey sport," I sang out. "Just because you run around wearing a three-thousand-dollar coat doesn't give you the right to trample people in the—"

He stopped me cold by turning around.

My first thought was an adolescent "Wow!" My second thought was, "What a pity." Because he was handsome. I mean photograph-like-a-million-bucks-from-any-angle-handsome. We're talking Mel Gibson blue eyes, thick dark hair, a jawline so square it was a cliché, great shoulders and chest, and a narrow waist. We're talking leading-man good looks. Except that he was too short. Not that all leading men are tall—there's a reason why Sigourney Weaver and Geena Davis work in low heels so much—but there is a cutoff point. The fellow standing in front of me was under it. No way you could get him through a love scene with an average-sized actress even if you put her in a trench. You'd have to keep them seated, or better yet, keep him horizontal . . . I pulled my mind back from its wanderings. And reminded myself that (a) I didn't produce soap operas anymore, and (b) this wasn't an actor I was planning to hire. This was a rude jerk with a taste for overpriced clothes.

He was looking at me. "My coat didn't cost three thousand dollars," he said finally, in a smoky baritone. It was a genuine, honest-to-God bedroom voice. If I'd still been casting hunks for *Bright Tomorrow,* I would have wept.

"Okay," I said. "It cost two thousand eight hundred and some change, retail. The point is—"

"How do you know?"

"Because we bought the same one for a character named Dirk Tarrow to wear on *Bright Tomorrow.* You think real people wear coats like that? Not outside a yuppie wet dream."

I felt I was finally hitting my stride with the zingers, but he didn't seem to notice. He was too busy staring at my knees in the shredded panty hose.

"You're hurt," he said. "What happened?"

I started to lose steam. It's hard to stay belligerent with someone who seems genuinely concerned about your infirmities.

"I fell."

On the other hand, I wasn't eager to admit that I'd taken a header over a Christmas decoration.

"On Park Avenue."

He didn't pursue it. "We should put some disinfectant on that scrape," he said. "Hop up on the desk. I know Teresa has a first-aid kit somewhere."

I hate having people take care of me. It makes me feel helpless. "That's okay . . ." I began, but he was already at my side.

"Up you go." Two steely hands grasped my waist, lifted me

easily, and deposited me on the desk. Well, I'd known from the shoulders that he worked out.

"Who are you, by the way?" he asked as he rummaged around in Teresa's desk.

From the doorway behind us Teresa said, "Her name is Angie DaVito. Angie, meet my brother, Patrick."

18

When I looked carefully I could see the family resemblance. Of course, Teresa was taller. But even if they hadn't shared eyes and mouths I'd have known they were related when they started to talk to each other. Most families have their own shorthand, I've discovered.

"Ma . . . ?" asked Teresa with a hint of a sigh.

Patrick nodded. "Midnight Mass."

"I've got paperwork, an interrogation . . ."

"Teresa . . ."

"I know, I know . . . Christmas."

At that moment I decided to insert myself into the dialogue. "You could hold off questioning me for a couple of days," I offered.

Teresa focused on me for the first time. "What did you do to yourself?" she asked.

"I tripped."

She waited. Unlike her sibling, I knew she would pursue it. So I told them what had happened. After I finished, brother and sister exchanged a look which made me hate them both a lot.

Patrick finished patching me up; then Teresa pulled out the little notepad she uses when she's questioning people, and he retired discreetly to the outer area. I guess as the son and grandson of a cop, he knew when to disappear. I'd been hoping he'd hang around for a while longer.

I wasn't looking forward to my interview with Teresa. I didn't know how much of the Robert saga Sammy had finally decided to tell. I was willing to cover for the kid, but it's hard to tell a good lie when you're flying blind.

However, Teresa let me off the hook on that one. "Samantha Jones has told me all about her relationship with Mr. Morton. Perhaps you might like to fill me in on what I don't know."

So I launched into an account of the argument I'd overheard when I was poking around the second soundstage.

"Obviously when Grace said, 'You know what I can do,' she meant she'd go to the tabloids again and tell them about Samantha having an affair with Robert," I said when I'd finished my narrative.

"Yes, I suppose that must have been it," said Teresa thoughtfully.

"Grace was blackmailing someone connected with the show. And whoever it was—" I stopped short. Sometimes things hit you a certain way. I remembered the darkness and the eerie silence in the soundstage. I remembered shivering in the cold.

"Whoever Grace was threatening . . . could have been the killer," I said slowly.

"That certainly is a good possibility."

"I was six yards away. I was alone in there with someone who may have committed murder."

It had been a long day. One that might be termed eventful. I hadn't had anything to eat since my breakfast bagel. I felt myself begin to shiver again. Teresa went to the door of her office. "Patrick," she called out. He materialized. "See if there's some hot coffee somewhere—Angie's cold."

"No I'm not," I said through chattering teeth. They both ignored me.

"Caffeine is not a good idea," said Patrick, eyeing me judiciously. "I'm afraid you'll have to settle for a yuppie wet dream." Two thousand eight hundred dollars and change worth of fine Italian tailoring dropped around my shoulders. My teeth immediately stopped the castanet imitation. What I hate about the shakes is, you have no control over when you have them and when you don't.

"Feeling better?" asked Patrick blandly.

"Thank you. I'm just fine," I said with what I hoped was great dignity.

They were back to ignoring me. "I think she's had enough for one evening," said Patrick.

"Just a few more questions and then you can drive her home," said Teresa.

"I said I was fine," I protested to no one in particular.

Teresa checked her notebook. "Angie, that story about Samantha and the young man, would it really have been so damaging to her mother's show?"

She'd put her finger on a question that had troubled me, too.

"I don't know," I said. "Obviously they all think it would be a disaster if it got out. And they do know their audience better than I do . . ."

"But you don't agree."

"The story would have been big news right after it broke, no doubt about that. It probably would have made the cover of *People*—unless they got lucky and Princess Di did something really weird that week. But I think they could have handled it—maybe even turned it around to their own advantage. I mean, none of that negative press ever hurt Roseanne." One look at her told me Teresa didn't know who I was talking about. She may be the only person in America who really does limit her television viewing to the news and educational programs on PBS. So before she could ask me who Roseanne was, I added hastily, "To answer your question—no, I don't think Samantha's little fling was such a big deal."

Teresa nodded. "Now let's talk about Felice Rovere. Why did she stay in New York when she was supposed to be in Connecticut getting ready for the holiday?"

"I haven't a clue."

"Does Samantha know?"

"She told me she didn't," I said carefully.

To my surprise Teresa didn't follow up on it. Instead she went back to the notebook, which I knew from the past was a device she used in an interrogation for rhythm and timing, not as a memory jog. Teresa O'Hanlon always knows what questions she's going to ask. "You were in the bathroom during the Christmas party when the doll was discovered, weren't you?" she asked. "Do you remember if anyone touched it?"

"Felice was going to, but then she backed off."

"You're sure no one brushed up against it accidentally."

"It wasn't the kind of thing you bump into. We all kept our distance from it. I don't think anyone touched it until I took it down later."

"You took it down?"

"When I cleaned up the bathroom. They didn't tell you?"

She paused. "No, but I probably should have known." She made a note—a real one this time. "Were you wearing black, Angie?"

"Am I a New York woman?"

"Was anyone else? How about Ms. Rovere?"

"Yes, she was wearing black too. It was a dinner suit. Designer quality, but I can't give you the name because it wasn't the kind of thing we bought much for *Bright Tomorrow* . . ." I realized I was rambling and stopped myself. "Why do you want to know?"

"I think that's all for now. Why don't you let Patrick drive you home?"

"Wait a minute . . ."

"We'll talk again, Angie."

I wanted to ask her why she was so interested in black evening clothes. But Teresa has a way of dismissing you that doesn't allow for argument. I stood up. Then sat down again—quickly and painfully. I turned to Patrick. "What did you do to my knee?" I demanded.

"You may have stiffened up a bit," he said.

"Patrick's car is right in front of the building," said Teresa. "Think you can make it?"

"Thanks, I'll get a cab."

"Perhaps that might not be the best idea," Patrick said gently. "Given what happens when you try to hail them."

I glared at him. He smiled sweetly.

"I wouldn't dream of putting you out," I said.

"Not at all. It's my pleasure."

I couldn't think of a way to refuse that wouldn't have made me sound like a petulant three-year-old. So I shrugged my acceptance. Which merely made me seem churlish.

"I'm not going to thank you for bringing me into this one, Angie," said Teresa as she walked us to the elevator, "but have a Merry Christmas anyway."

"You too," I said.

At my side I could feel Patrick freeze. "You called Teresa in on this case?" he demanded.

"Patrick, mind your own business," she said.

———

In the elevator Patrick said nothing. And more nothing. Finally I'd had it. "I called your sister because I know her and I trust her. Is something wrong with that?"

"Not from your point of view. But the last thing Teresa needs right now is another high-profile case."

"Why?"

"She's a woman who's already gone too far too fast in the police department for some people—there are guys on the force who still see a man out of a job when they look at a woman in a uniform. And these boys are not happy when a female, who should be home having kids as far as they're concerned, grabs all the showy cases and the headlines."

So that was why she'd seemed so hesitant on the phone.

"She didn't grab. I called."

"That's beside the point. They're going to make it rough on her this time. They'll make her pay for the spotlight."

"That never occurred to me."

"Yeah."

When he was cross, he tightened his jaw. Which just made it look even more ridiculously square and perfect.

By the time we reached the street, Patrick had managed to shake his crankiness. Being a flash-in-the-pan type myself, I approved—God save me from those who mope. He then won additional points by opening the car door for me, which is the kind of gallantry that doesn't happen too often in my postfem-lib circle.

The interior of his car was as plush as I'd imagined it would be. It was also perfumed with a sweet, yeasty fragrance that made my empty stomach growl audibly.

"Something smells wonderful," I said, to cover the sound. I hoped I wasn't drooling.

Patrick lifted a glitzy laminated shopping bag from the passenger seat and stowed it in the back. "It's fresh stollen. I always bring a couple of loaves to the family for Christmas morning." I remembered that Teresa had told me he was the guiding force behind a wildly successful bakery.

"That's right, Teresa told me—you're Mother . . . somebody."

Patrick winced slightly. "Mother Maggie," he said. "The image consultant told me the name would have recognition value. By the time I got rid of her, the name had stuck."

It served him right for using an image consultant in the first place, I thought but did not say. After all, the man had just opened my car door. "I think it's a real nice name," I told him, hoping it didn't sound as lame to him as it did to me. I turned around to look at the fancy red and gold bag, which must have upped the price of his baked goods by a considerable chunk. "Nice bag, too."

He looked at me with concern. "Are you okay?" he asked.

"Sure. Why?"

He seemed to be considering something. Then he asked slowly, "What would you say if I told you that Mother Maggie supplies the pastries for three separate chains of coffeehouses in Manhattan?"

"You mean those little hole-in-the-wall places that have been taking over my neighborhood and charging three-fifty a cup for swill called hazelnut mochaccino and chocolate raspberry decaf? Those pretentious, loathsome—" I broke off because Patrick had started to chuckle to himself. "What?"

"Just running a little reality check."

"Setting me up is more like it. You knew what I'd say."

He didn't deny it, but he grinned at me. I couldn't help it, I grinned back. After which we drove in silence for a while. Which was very strange for me. Usually silence makes me nervous. It's a performer thing—dead air is the enemy. Anything, including inane babble, is preferable. But with Patrick somehow the quiet seemed okay. Actually it was better than okay. It was . . . comfortable. I leaned back in my soft velvety seat and let myself relax. And I felt how deep-in-the-bones tired I was. Which wasn't surprising, since the clock on his dashboard said 12:45.

"You're going to miss Midnight Mass," I said sleepily.

"I know. I didn't expect to make it. Ma just wanted to be sure Teresa didn't skip the holiday again."

"Does she often do that?"

"Since Bobby died, she tries to."

It made me think. About Teresa cheerfully working through Christmas Eve so she wouldn't have to think about Bobby. And Grace Shipley, who wouldn't have any more Christmas Eves ever again. And me, running around New York when I could be baking phallic cookies in Connecticut . . .

"Angie," said a voice from far away. "Angie, this is your apartment building." I came back slowly. "You dozed off," said Patrick, who wasn't far away at all. In fact, he was leaning over me. If I wanted to, I could reach out and trace the little lines in the corners of his eyes. He smiled. "Are you awake now?" I nodded, still groggy. He had a nice smile. He got out of the car and went around to open my door for me. He moved well too. Like an athlete—what sports did you play when you were that short? I wondered. A voice in the back of my mind murmured dreamily that short though he was, he still had a couple of inches on me.

That woke me up fast. I knew that voice. It had gotten me

into trouble before. I sat upright so I could silence it before it got out of hand. No way, I told it sharply. We are not going to even think about falling for Teresa O'Hanlon's brother. For one thing, we are still trying to grow scar tissue over the wounds we sustained in our last serious relationship. But more important, this pint-sized Adonis—who, if he is still unattached at his age in the city of Manhattan, represents a statistical miracle—is too well built and well dressed. This is a glamour boy. Think actor without Equity card. We do not fall in love with actors. We are mature.

I got my stiff and aching body out of the car and stuck out my wounded hand briskly. "Thank you for the lift, Patrick," I said. "And Merry Christmas."

We shook hands, which hurt a lot more than I'd expected, and I turned to go. "Wait a sec," he said. He reached into the back seat of his car and pulled out a loaf of stollen wrapped in gold and red tissue paper. He handed it to me. "Merry Christmas, Angie," he said.

"Define mature," said my inner voice.

It seemed as if it had been a million years since I'd last seen my apartment. Usually I love coming home, no matter how late it is, or where I've been. My apartment is my fortress. But at that moment it just seemed dark. And lonely. In the corner of the living room the ornaments glittered on my snake plant. Next year, I decided, I'd spring for a string of lights.

The stollen gave me a moment of truth. Ever since I starved off my baby fat in my mid-twenties, I've trained myself not to eat sweets. On the other hand, it was Christmas Eve. I sat in the dark and polished off most of the loaf before I went to bed.

19

Naturally the media blackout on the murder didn't hold through the next morning. I grabbed a newspaper in Port Authority on my way to the bus—again—and found the story on the front page next to a Christmas heart-warmer about the late shopper who'd delivered her baby in our twentieth-century version of the manger—the ladies' room at Radio City Music Hall.

Cee Gee's lawyer had been right about the timing of the murder being a lucky break, because the tone of the article was remarkably restrained. It simply stated that the body of Grace Shipley, longtime friend and staff member of talk show hostess Cee Gee Jones, had been found in the Park Avenue co-op owned by Ms. Jones. The deceased had died of a gunshot wound in the chest. The discovery had been made early on Christmas Eve.

Ms. Jones, the article went on to say, had not been back to her apartment since leaving it right after breakfast. She and her executive producer, Victoria Townsend-Stuart, had spent the morning, as they did every year on the day before Christmas, distributing the food purchased by Cee Gee's Food Fund (For Our Less Fortunate Friends) to the city's shelters. In a charmingly homey touch George Stuart, Ms. Townsend-Stuart's husband, had driven them on their rounds in a van. As usual the event had been recorded by a camera crew from a popular local news show called *Live at Five*. Ms. Jones and Ms. Townsend-Stuart were slated to be the guests on the show that evening.

"We go on *Live at Five* to talk about Cee Gee's food drive every Christmas Eve," Ms. Townsend-Stuart was quoted as saying, speaking for Ms. Jones, who was too distraught over the recent tragedy to be interviewed. "It's Cee Gee's way of reminding everyone that there is still time to help those who are in need."

By noon the mission of mercy was complete and Mr. Stuart left in the van for the Townsend-Stuart manse in Connecticut. His wife and Ms. Jones went on to their offices at Ms. Jones's brand-new studio complex on the West Side.

"Cee Gee and I don't really work the day before Christmas," the story further quoted Ms. Townsend-Stuart. "The staff is off and the studio is closed. We stay in the city because of the *Live at Five* appearance. It cuts into our own holiday, but that kind of personal generosity is typical of Cee Gee. No sacrifice is too great for a great cause."

Or great publicity, I thought. But I read on eagerly.

According to the article, Ms. Townsend-Stuart had left the studio a little before two o'clock to take care of some last-minute Christmas shopping, while Ms. Jones stayed in her office working with an assistant. Ms. Townsend-Stuart then returned to the office at about four o'clock, in time to go with Ms. Jones to CBS for the TV appearance at five.

It was right after the news show, while they were still at the station, that they got a frantic phone call from Ms. Jones's daughter, who had discovered the body of Ms. Shipley in the upstairs bathroom of Ms. Jones's Park Avenue duplex.

A preliminary report from the coroner placed the time of

death at between twelve and three-thirty that afternoon. The police were investigating the crime. They had several leads but were not willing to discuss the case any further for the present.

I folded the paper and stuffed it into a shopping bag with the remains of the stollen. For the first time since I'd heard about the possibility of working for Cee Gee Jones, I was excited. Which was not a good sign—as both Teresa and Freddie would have told me. But it wasn't my fault. Could I help it if murder—and the solving of it—seemed to be a leitmotiv in my life these days?

I wasn't the only one who was fascinated by the murder. It was topic A for the entire weekend. Even Connie got into it. Despite intense grilling from the kids, I refused to discuss my impromptu trip into the city, my connection with Cee Gee Jones, or my bruises. I also threatened to maim any family member who mentioned these topics to friends, no matter how dear and trusted. It was a smart move because New Milford had gone crazy. The fact that the actual killing had taken place in New York didn't seem to matter; the area adopted the crime as its own. People drove up to Kent to watch the press shivering in the frozen pasture outside Cee Gee's house, or to catch a glimpse of Hamlet's Violet VI frolicking with the cook and the housekeeper on the front lawn. No one else was in residence, but that didn't seem to dampen the general enthusiasm. Anyone who had watched even one episode of *Lau and Order* was on the phone discussing forensic techniques. Neighbors dropped in on each other to drink coffee and speculate about possible motives. For the first time in recorded history, Connie's Lane cake was consumed down to the last chopped raisin by the end of Boxing Day. And we were all glued to the tube.

Mark and Manuela, the two hosts of the weekend edition of *AM Live*, kicked off the marathon coverage.

"Manuela, the police are really floored by this case," said Mark. "Normally they'd be able to get a list of people who had gone into Cee Gee's apartment building at or around the time of the shooting from the doorman, which would be a big help in finding the perp."

"Did you say 'perp,' Mark? Is that police talk?" Manuela joshed. Mark did a playful moment. "Okay, okay, you caught me. But seriously, this is an *AM Live* exclusive."

At the sacred word "exclusive," Manuela sobered up right away. "You're absolutely right, Mark. And now to continue our exclusive *AM Live* coverage, we go to our reporter Kimberly Dane on the scene at Cee Gee Jones's Manhattan apartment. Hi there, Kim."

A blue-eyed, blue-lipped young woman wearing a photogenic coat which could not have provided any real warmth appeared on the screen.

"Hi Manuela. Here's our exclusive *AM Live* story about the faulty security at Cee Gee Jones's luxury Park Avenue co-op. It seems that the front doorman at this apartment building likes to play the ponies. The co-op board has reprimanded him many times for placing bets with his bookie on the house telephone. So he sneaks out every day at two o'clock and uses a public phone on Lexington Avenue." A shot of a generic New York public phone appeared on the screen while Manuela enthused, "So the plot thickens."

"Exactly," said Kim, sending puffs of frozen breath into the camera lens. "Because while the doorman was away from his desk anyone could have gone up to the penthouse. So when

Ms. Shipley arrived at the building claiming to have a two-thirty appointment with Ms. Jones . . ."

"The doorman didn't know if Cee Gee was up there, or someone else was." Mark stole her thunder and her punch line.

Kimberly looked a little sour as she said, "You got it, Mark."

"It gives me goose bumps just to think about it, Kimberley," offered Manuela.

The tabloid shows pushed the story forward.

The natty Britisher on *Hard Story* was salivating visibly. "We have learned from exclusive *Hard Story* sources that Ms. Shipley told the doorman that Ms. Jones had asked her to come to the penthouse," he said. "Since the doorman knew Ms. Shipley was a regular visitor of Ms. Jones's, he allowed her to go up even though there was no answer when he buzzed the apartment. He admits that his major concern was to avoid drawing attention to the fact that he had been away from his desk." The reporter paused dramatically. "Now, according to the doorman, Ms. Shipley said Ms. Jones left a message on her answering machine summoning her to the apartment. Yet when police went to Ms. Shipley's apartment they were not able to find any such message on the tape in the machine."

"So what? Grace could have erased the message after she heard it, you jerk," I said out loud.

The poor man's David Frost snuck a peek at his notes. "Police are checking the tape for the possibility of an erased message," he said.

"I told you so," said I.

"Why is Aunt Angie yelling at the TV, Mommy?" asked Arnie junior.

"Because Aunt Angie spends too much time alone and will not see a therapist to deal with her problem with commitment," said his mother.

But I was too busy simultaneously hating the media feeding frenzy and channel surfing for more information to answer her. And the tabloids kept the story rolling.

Dick, the male anchor on *Inside Info*, had obviously spent his formative years watching game shows—he wanted desperately to be hosting *Jeopardy*. His female counterpart, Beryl, wanted to be Barbara Walters.

Dick jumped in first. "Well, Beryl, after the murder, the killer had to leave the building, which meant going past the doorman's desk. This would have been a golden opportunity for the doorman to redeem himself. But this killer was clever."

"Clever is the word, Dick," Beryl said gravely. She was doing early Barbara—from the era when she used to interview Henry Kissinger. "Somehow the killer knew that the doormen in this building change shifts at three-thirty, and according to our exclusive *Inside Info* interview with the building superintendent, there is always some confusion during the changeover. There can be no doubt that the killer made his or her escape during those few brief moments."

"Diabolical," said Dick happily.

It was the former Miss Black America, anchor of *Happening Today*, who broke the final scoop of the day. "Police sources say a doll which bore a striking resemblance to Ms. Jones was found hanging in Ms. Jones's bathroom three days before the murder. Something which looked like a toy bullet was buried in its chest. Unfortunately we can't show you the real thing. However, here is a facsimile." A shot of a doll with its face blanked out flashed on the screen. It looked suspiciously like Barbie to me.

"Black fibers from an unknown source were found in the hair of this strange figure. No one knows whether the use of this image of Cee Gee Jones was part of a sexual fantasy . . .

". . . a satanic rite . . ." Beryl told Dick.

". . . the work of alien creatures from planets unknown to man . . ." intoned Great Britain's gift to American journalism.

"So that's why Teresa was so hung up on black clothes," I said to Ralphie, who was the only member of the family still hanging in with me and the remote control. "But that must mean she's not sure it was Grace who set up the hanging doll." I turned off the tube and began to pace. Hoping for a game, my faithful companion scrambled to his feet along with me.

The idea that someone other than Grace might have staged the scene in the bathroom intrigued me. Townie and the gang simply assumed she had done it. But it seemed like such a clumsy way to get revenge, and Grace had demonstrated that she could be remarkably efficient in that area.

"So what if Grace didn't do it, Ralphie? Then who did? And why?"

Ralphie thumped his tail on the floor vigorously. In canine-speak it meant, "I'm enthralled with your brilliance, now throw a toy for me."

"Teresa's obviously going after the fibers they found in the doll's hair. But I think there may be an easier way."

Ralphie cocked his head to indicate, "I'm hanging on your every word, how about a cookie?"

"I think someone should talk to the makeup artist. Because of the fake blood. If you work in a television studio, a logical place to get fake blood, or to find out how to make it, would be the makeup room, wouldn't it?"

Ralphie gave me the nose nudge that says, "I'm doing my best, but your idea of fun is starting to bore the hell out of me."

I sat down and scratched him behind the ears while I pondered. I didn't know the name of Cee Gee's makeup person. And I didn't have any of my union phone books out in the boondocks. However . . .

I got up abruptly, dumping Ralphie's head out of my lap. "Sorry, buddy," I said. "Got to make a phone call."

Ralphie flopped on the floor with a disgruntled "oof" that was designed to let me know how deeply I'd failed him after all the devotion he'd lavished on me. He really was Connie's dog.

I felt a little hesitant about making long-distance calls from Connie's phone. Not that anyone would have minded, but Arnie's idea of a kicky way to spend a free Saturday is reviewing every charge on his bill. So some day in late January I might have to explain myself. And then I'd have to face one of those sisterly conversations which begin, "Angie, if you had kids and a home of your own, you wouldn't feel this need to meddle in things that don't concern you . . ."

However, I was too hot on the trail to stop. It took me about fifteen minutes to figure out how to use my telephone credit card, but I finally got it together to call Vinnie Santucci's house on Long Island. I was betting that Joey, as was the custom of his generation, had chosen not to move out of his parents' comfortable home with the regular meals and his mother to do his laundry. I lucked out. Not only was Joey in residence, he answered the phone.

After the amenities, and a mutual expressions of curiosity about the recent tragedy, I made my request. Joey told me I was looking for one John-Anne Belk. He gave me a phone number and a home address located in the heart of the gallery district in SoHo. But it seemed to me that he was a little reluctant to give out the information. "Just remember John-Anne's good people, Angie," he said cryptically, as we signed off.

I'd been planning to call Ms. Belk and suggest that we get together, but after talking to Joey I decided to wing it. Why, I wasn't quite sure. But then that was the point of winging it.

Feeling pleased with myself because I'd taken some action, I addressed the dog. "I'm onto something, Ralphie," I said. "I know I am."

Ralphie, whose short-term memory isn't all that it might be, forgot that he was mad at me and leapt up on the couch to reward me with fervent, drooling kisses.

20

On the morning of the 27th I insisted on going back to the city even though Connie pointed out repeatedly that I didn't have to work that day. We finally compromised on my hour of departure—later than I wanted, earlier than she did—and I arrived in the city with plenty of time to make the trip down to John-Anne's loft on West Broadway. She was at home and not thrilled about an unexpected visitor. However, she did ask me in and offered me some herb tea, which she called a tisane. While she was boiling water in her kitchen, I wandered around the rest of her home. It was a warm, airy space with bare brick walls, original hardwood floors, and furniture covered with bright fabrics which looked hand-loomed.

"So how can I help you, Ms. DaVito?" she asked warily.

"Angie, please."

"Angie," she agreed, without a corresponding offer for me to call her John-Anne. She was an attractive young woman with golden-brown skin. She wore an emerald nose stud and cornrows decorated with matching green beads. Her colorful pants outfit was native to somewhere not of this continent, but her accent was homegrown in the borough of Brooklyn.

Since she clearly wasn't going to give me any help making small talk, I plunged in. "Ms. Belk, I know this is going to sound strange, but I'd like to know if you keep fake blood in

your makeup kit. Or at the studio. I know there's not much
call for it on the job, but—"

To my surprise, she laughed. A big relief laugh. "Is that
what this is about?" she asked. "The fake blood?"

"Yes, what did you think?"

The laugh died. She looked stricken. Like she'd screwed
up somehow. "I don't know what I thought . . . I mean . . . that
was stupid of me, wasn't it? Of course you'd want to know
about the blood. You were there, you saw the doll." She
pulled herself together and smiled. Obviously she thought
she'd bailed herself out.

"How did you know I was in the bathroom that night?"

Her smile vanished. We were back to stricken.

"I heard about it," she said.

"How?"

"The story has been all over the news."

"Was my name mentioned? Because I've been all but glued
to the television for the past twenty-four hours and I didn't
hear it once."

"Now that I think about it, I heard about the doll at the
studio, the day after Cee Gee's party."

But at that time Townie, Cee Gee, Felice, Samantha,
George, and I—and possibly Grace—were the only ones who
knew about the scene in the bathroom. John-Anne was a lousy
liar.

"Who told you?" I asked.

"What's it to you?" She was getting hostile—next move,
she'd throw me out. I beat a hasty retreat.

"Actually, that doesn't matter to me. I'm only interested in
the fake blood."

"Why?" It wasn't a friendly question.

"It's protection for the show. I'm the new senior producer and we just want to be sure there's nothing out there that the supermarket rags could twist and use to hurt us imagewise. You know how it is." Unlike John-Anne, I am a wonderful liar, so my story came off the tongue smooth as silk. She relaxed a little.

"I do keep some fake blood in my kit, but I checked after I heard about . . . the incident, and none of it was gone."

"Can you remember if anyone on the show ever asked you about professional makeup outlets where they might buy fake blood?"

"No, but . . ."

"How about a formula for making it?"

"No, but people on the show wouldn't have to."

"Why not?"

"That's what I'm trying to tell you. Anyone who works at the studio would know how to make the blood, because last Halloween Cee Gee did this cutesy show she called 'Making Your Own Goblins.' I was one of her guests—she loves to use what she calls her 'Cee Gee family' because she thinks it makes her look warm—and I showed the audience how to make fake blood."

"Oh."

"I told all of this to the police."

Damn. "So the police have talked to you?"

"Yeah. Nice-looking African-American cop. Great dimples."

There's no use pretending I wasn't miffed. I'd thought the fake blood was my lead. Well, it served me right for even thinking I could compete with the people who did this for a living.

I made a few more minutes of polite conversation, swallowed the last of my tea, which tasted the way the stuff Mama used to rub on our chests when we had colds smelled, and took my leave.

As I headed uptown I got over my snit and started reviewing the reactions and behavior of John-Anne Belk. Obviously someone had told her about the discovery of the doll. But who? And why was she so nervous about it? And had Hank picked up on this interesting little sideline when he questioned her, or was this one all mine? Not that I was trying to compete with the cops or anything . . .

21

"You got a visitor," said my doorman when I walked into the lobby of my building. He pointed to an extremely blond person, swathed in scarves and carrying a small cardboard carton, who was standing in front of the elevators. She turned as I walked toward her.

"Samantha?"

She tugged at her blond wig. "Your doorman is one suspicious cocksucker, you know? I mean, if he treats all your nieces the way he treated me . . ."

"You're not my niece."

"He doesn't know that."

"He knows a phony when he sees one. Why have you gotten yourself up like something out of a bad Humphrey Bogart movie?"

"Who?"

I decided not to let her ignorance depress me.

"Does anyone know you're here, Samantha?"

"Of course not. Why the fuck do you think I'm dressed like something out of a bad Humphrey whoever movie? Mama's lawyers have turned the apartment into a prison. I can't even use the phone without clearing it with six people. And with those scumbags from the press hanging around outside . . . I've been going batshit."

"Come upstairs to my apartment," I said.

Now she'll tell me what she's been holding back, I thought as we rode up in the elevator. Teresa, eat your heart out.

"Funky," said Samantha as she toured my humble abode. "Where's the kitchen?"

"There."

She looked at me in disbelief. "I thought only guys had kitchens like that," she said. I let her wander for a while. Clearly she wasn't ready to talk. She stopped in front of my mirror and patted her head nervously. "Do you like the wig?"

"Your own hair is prettier," I evaded.

"Yeah, well, I was wondering about going platinum, but now I think I'd look like homemade shit."

It was a wise decision. Some of us are not born to be blondes.

"Samantha . . ."

"You want me to tell you why I'm here." There was a pause. Then she placed the carton she'd been clutching on the beat-up counter which serves as my kitchen/dining room table and room divider.

"You said I had to tell you everything."

"And I meant it."

"Take a look at this crap."

The box contained two items, both of which had been sealed in plastic freezer bags. I lifted out the smaller of the two.

"It isn't real," said Samantha. But it was a very realistic plastic replica of a human heart. I took it out of the bag.

"I think it's from a kid's game," said Samantha.

"But why . . . ?"

"Look at it."

I did. And I saw what she was talking about. In the center of the heart was a round hole. In it was wedged a toy bullet. Red paint had been spattered around the wound to simulate blood.

I put it down carefully and took out the second bag.

"It's Mama's book," said Sam softly. And indeed it was a copy of Cee Gee's best-selling autobiography. From the outside it seemed to be in good shape. Even the jacket was pristine. Then I opened it. Someone had painstakingly pasted an official-looking document over the third page, covering the dedication to cherished Samantha, who was the source of all the author's courage and wisdom.

The document was a little too big, so it had been folded tidily around the edges to fit the page exactly. I unfolded it. And realized I was looking at a copy of a death certificate. There had been a name on the original, and other pertinent information. All of that had been whited out and in its place new information had been typed before the copying. Cee Gee Jones was the new name. The cause of death was listed as a gunshot wound in the heart. Dribbles and splotches of red paint decorated the thing.

Samantha and I looked at each other.

"Where did those things come from, Samantha?"

"They were left in Mama's office at the studio. The heart came first. Then about two weeks later it was the book. Townie told Mama to throw them away. I could tell Mama didn't want to—I think she wanted to show them to the cops because by then she'd had it with Grace, you know? So she brought them home while she tried to decide. But Townie kept on her ass until she tossed them. I got them out of the trash in the basement."

"Townie and your mother thought Grace was responsible for this stuff?"

She nodded.

"Just because she was fired?"

"Grace was pissed big-time about the way they were canning her," she said.

"But this was an over-the-top reaction. Getting fired in this business is an occupational hazard. No matter who you are. We all know it can happen."

"Not Grace. She thought they'd never get rid of her, no matter what."

"Why did she think that? I got the idea she wasn't exactly well loved."

"She was on everyone's shit list. But it didn't matter."

"Why not?"

She hesitated. "I don't know."

"Come on, Samantha."

She picked up her purse and began going through it. After a second she produced a pack of cigarettes. "You mind?" she asked.

"Very much."

She put them away with a sigh. "I quit a year ago, but with all the shit that's been going down . . ."

"Samantha, stop stalling."

"All right. You've got to understand, I don't *know* anything . . . but I . . . Well, it's just this feeling I have."

"What kind of feeling?"

"That something's wrong. Part of it is Townie. She's losing it, I think. When she and Mama were fighting about firing Grace, Townie begged Mama not to. And Townie doesn't beg."

"So Townie and your mom disagreed and your mom won. Don't tell me that never happens."

"But this time it was like Townie was scared. And Mama was too, just not as much. Felice wasn't happy about it either."

"They were scared about firing Grace?"

"Yes, but that wasn't the only reason." She paused, searching hard for the right words. "Something's been weirding out Mama and Townie and Felice for a long time. Grace knew about it too, I think."

"And you have no idea what 'it' is?"

She shook her head. "I just know it's something that's been going on for a long time. Nobody talks about it, but it's there—it's like it's in the air. And I've always been afraid of it because it scares them so much."

"How long have you felt this way?"

"As long as I can remember. I think it started in the old days down in Georgia when Mama first started to get hot."

"You were a baby then."

"I know. That's why I can't tell you what it was that happened. Just that I know all the shit didn't start with this thing with me and Robert, no matter how hard Townie tries to blame me." She looked at me defiantly, but her eyes were welling up. "Townie wishes I'd just disappear."

"I'm sure she doesn't . . ." I began, but stopped short. Something told me she knew what she was talking about. She blinked hard to get the tears under control.

"I never meant to hurt Mama," she said quietly.

"Of course you didn't."

"Townie has hated me all my life because somehow I'm tied up with whatever's wrong."

With most teenagers, I'd have dismissed the statement as

adolescent melodrama. But Sammy wasn't the melodramatic type. Underneath all the attitude, she was essentially a prosaic little soul—earthy, practical, and not the type to create high drama where there was none.

"Sammy, did you ever try to talk to Townie about any of this?"

"Give me a fucking break."

"What about your mother?"

She gave me the classic look of agents, managers, and all those whose job it is to handle stars. It's an expression that is part indulgence and part frazzle, with just a suggestion of contempt thrown in. "Mama doesn't deal with negative vibes."

"But you're her daughter."

"That doesn't matter. We can't upset her." It was an article of faith, stated simply, without self-pity or resentment. "Besides," she added, "right now she's off the wall enough over Felice."

"Felice?"

"Her alibi sucks. I'm no help because I was with Robert when Grace was . . . you know."

"Murdered. Where was Felice?"

There was a pause. "She told the police she was doing some last-minute Christmas shopping."

"Do you believe that?"

There was another, longer pause. "It's what she says."

"That's not what I asked you."

"Look, all I know is, whatever Felice does when she sneaks off, Valentine's Day and her birthday are big deals. And last New Year's when she was supposed to be visiting her dear old mama on the farm, she came back with four champagne corks, a whole bunch of those little paper umbrellas they put in those pukey fruit drinks you get in the tropics, and a T-shirt from someplace in Jamaica."

I considered asking how she'd discovered all of this and then decided that I didn't want to know.

"So she has a lover. What's wrong with that?"

"Everything if he works for the show. Townie has always had rules about people at the studio getting it on together. And now after what happened with Grace and me and the prick, she's a total madwoman about it."

"I assume you haven't told the police about Felice's travel souvenirs."

She gave me a grin I liked better than her mother's more famous version, and shook her head vigorously.

"Have you told them about the heart and the book?"

This time she shook her head without the smile. "No cops," she said decisively.

"Those things are evidence in a murder case."

"So? I wouldn't even have them if I hadn't gotten them out of the garbage. If Townie knew, she'd go ballistic. And Mama too. Mama's stressed enough, no way I'm going to make it worse for her."

She looked so fierce—and so vulnerable.

"Sammy . . ." I began gently.

"Plus, the cops might decide Mama was trying to hide something when she tossed the book and the heart. And if the cops didn't, the fucking tabloids would. That's why I showed you the stuff, Angie. I thought you'd know what to do. I thought you'd help me."

"I'm trying to—by giving you the best advice I can."

"Shit." She retrieved her coat and began rewinding her scarves around her neck. "I shouldn't have come. I gotta get the fuck out of here."

"Sammy, wait. If you won't tell the police, at least give that stuff to your mother's lawyers. They'll know what to do."

That seemed to resonate better. She turned to me. "You think?" she asked.

"Let them decide. That's what they're paid for."

After a second she nodded. Clearly she trusted people who were being paid outrageous sums of money more than those who had merely taken an oath to uphold the law. Well, who could blame her?

22

I've found that the most important questions are often the ones that don't occur to you until it's too late to ask them. So naturally as soon as Samantha left, I came up with many. The first had to do with something she'd said about not being allowed to wear makeup because she was illegitimate and Townie was worried about Cee Gee's image. Cee Gee Jones had always been very open about her marital status—she was single—at the time of Sammy's birth. It was part of her legend. In fact, she'd first announced it to the world on her show. I didn't know the particulars of the story, but I knew there had been some sort of highly emotional incident with a guest who was also a single mother.

So why was Townie uptight about it? Or was Townie's alleged concern a figment of Samantha's imagination? And why had Townie begged Cee Gee not to fire Grace? Was there really some bit of history between this female triumvirate dating back to those early Georgia days—some secret that bound them together? Or had Samantha dreamed up that one, too?

I was too restless to sit, so I nuked dinner and roamed around the apartment for a bit, picking things up and putting them down while I ate. Since the big puzzle seemed to be out of reach, I tried focusing on a smaller, more contained one. Like the mystery of Felice's unknown love, which was such a big secret that she was willing to lie to the police in order to keep it that way. I couldn't believe that she'd be driven to such lengths simply because her sweetie worked on *Cee Gee!* After all, not even Townie could hope to keep sex completely off limits in a television studio. No, something else was going on—maybe Felice was in the process of breaking up a marriage with four kids. Or maybe . . . I ran down the list of all the people I'd met in the past few days. And had one of those flashes of insight that are so disturbing to Connie and the people who employ me.

It took two minutes to hunt down the phone number. Naturally, no one was home. The message I left on the answering machine was short and simple. "Felice Rovere is being a fool," I said, "and she could get herself in real trouble. She needs your help." I figured that should do it.

After that, since I seemed to be in the phoning mode, I checked in with my trusty answering service, StarsAnswrFone. I am the only person I know whose phone is not answered by an electronic gadget—partly because I hate them, but mostly because gadgets do not, so far as I know, make morning wake-up calls. I need a living, breathing human to nag me into consciousness every day.

"Your agent left a message to remind you that you're having lunch at the Russian Tea Room tomorrow to celebrate your new job," said the operator. "And may I add the congratulations of all of us here at StarsAnswrFone, Ms. DaVito?" I told her she could. StarsAnswrFone prides itself on these little personal touches—and of course, a customer who is being paid can continue to pay for her answering service.

"You also had a call from a Patrick Gallagher," she said—which immediately caused my stomach do the same flip it did when, at age fifteen, I clapped eyes on a sixteen-year-old heartthrob named Paul Dadario at the mixer between Holy Angel's School for Girls and St. Michael's Catholic Military Academy. I remember not enjoying the sensation much back then—and time and experience have done nothing to change my point of view. I tried to console myself with the upside: at least now I knew Teresa's maiden name.

"It was nothing urgent," the operator went on. "Mr. Gallagher just wanted to know if you were okay and hoped you were enjoying your holiday."

At first I decided not to call back. After all, he hadn't left his phone number. Then I told myself that I owed him a thank-you for the stollen, and calling was just a matter of being polite.

There are times when I tell myself the most amazing garbage. Worse, there are times when I believe it.

The Manhattan telephone directory lists about two hundred Gallaghers. I gave myself exactly one shot at finding him. To lengthen the odds, I picked the only Patrick Gallagher in my zip code. I figured if we were neighbors he'd have mentioned it when he brought me home.

He answered on the fourth ring.

"Why didn't you tell me you lived six blocks away from me?" I demanded after I'd gotten over the initial shock of making contact.

"I did. But you were asleep at the time."

"Oh." I could feel an endless pause starting to develop. "The stollen was really great. That's why I called. To tell you how great it was. Really great." I hate the way a little sexual attraction can turn me into a blithering fifteen-year-old. Still. After all this time. Then I heard a voice that sounded like mine say, "In fact, I'd like to take you out to dinner to say thank you."

"When?" he asked.

The evil spirit that had taken over my vocal cords answered, "How about tomorrow night? Around sevenish?" I never use bullshit words like "sevenish." He didn't seem to notice.

"I'll come by to pick you up," he said.

After we'd signed off it occurred to me that I probably should have offered to pick him up. The etiquette in these matters has always seemed a little vague to me. The truth is, I don't ask men out to dinner often—or, I'm ashamed to admit, with any real ease. I try to be nonchalant about it. But I have a feeling it's something you should start doing when you're very young. And it helps if you hit puberty after Doris Day stopped making feature films.

That night I had one of my anxiety dreams. I have a couple of old standards which my subconscious hauls out whenever the going gets rough. A favorite features me being forced to sing the lead in *La Traviata* without ever having learned it. When I get center stage I realize that my costume, while being historically accurate, is made of see-through plastic. I tossed and turned through this oldie but goody, and then segued into some images that were new and disturbing. When I woke up at three A.M., all I could remember was a voice telling me to "peel the onion," a doll which turned into a puppet, and a lot of people floating around wearing Halloween masks. Clearly it was a dream loaded with significance. What the hell it meant was beyond me.

I was up early the next morning thanks to StarsAnswrFone. After making sure that I was awake—which means I can recite the day of the week, my own name, and that of my president—the operator asked if there was anything else she could do for me.

"Not unless you can recommend an expensive restaurant which doesn't have indirect lighting," I growled. It wasn't fair of me. She wasn't programmed to handle an actual conversation. I apologized and hung up.

However, I did have a serious problem. Having offered to wine and dine Patrick, I now had to find the proper spot in which to do it. I don't keep track of the trendy eateries in my city, but I had a feeling that my usual hangout—a nice Italian place called Tony's which has been operating out of the same basement since Tony's grandfather came to this country in the twenties—wouldn't be Patrick's style. Fortunately, I have an impeccable source of information on all things hot and happening. I called Evie.

Evie McFidden is the Director of Client Relations at one of the biggest talent agencies in New York. It is her job to cater to the whims of the visiting celebs repped by her organization. With a flip of her gigantic Rolodex she can put you onto the best of anything in New York—from dog walkers to plastic surgeons to handmade chocolates. Once, she redecorated a client's apartment in three days while simultaneously putting the woman's mother in a nursing home. Needless to say, she knows every restaurant in Manhattan.

"Stella," she declared after I'd explained what I wanted. "It's a new place in Chelsea. Fabulous menu without being too foodie, just enough attitude to be interesting, great ambience. Want me to book it? I'll get a better table than you can."

"Please, Evie," I said unhappily. In my experience, great ambience in a restaurant always means indirect lighting.

23

I guess it's unfair of me to blame Donna Karan for everything that happened from that point on, but I do. Because if I hadn't owned one of her dresses—a red jersey number with just the right amount of cling—I would have gone shopping. Normally my wardrobe doesn't include the kind of hot little item you toss on for an evening at a place like Stella. But I knew there was no way I'd ever buy anything to top the Donna Karan because I would never have spent that kind of money on an article of clothing for myself.

The dress had been purchased for one of the actresses on *Bright Tomorrow*, who wore it once for a crucial fifteen-minute seduction scene. After which, since it couldn't be seen again on the show, we offered to let her buy it at the phenomenally reduced rate we always offered our performers. She declined on the grounds that red was an aggressive color which inhibited her spiritual flow. Since I don't have a spiritual flow that I'm aware of, and it was my size, I grabbed it.

Which explains why that morning before my lunch with Freddie, instead of racing around the city driving saleswomen crazy, I had time on my hands. Time in which to brood about the early days on Cee Gee's talk show down in Georgia, and Samantha's feeling that something was wrong. And I had time to do some research. Thanks to Donna.

I chose the Library for the Performing Arts at Lincoln Center as my resource—it's the best place in the city for all forms of entertainment-based information. And the staff is very patient with show biz types who are not adept at the Dewey decimal system.

The Billy Rose Theatre Collection is on the third floor. Before entering it, one must first surrender all purses, shopping bags, briefcases, coats with big pockets, or anything else in which a thief might smuggle out books or research material. It makes me sad because I can remember when this kind of security wasn't necessary. The librarian was delighted to be of service—especially when he read my employer's name on my requisition slip. "Cee Gee is God," he said, adding in an excited whisper, "Are you working on the . . . you know . . . the case?"

I gave him a loaded glance.

He raced off to take care of my request personally, and in no time at all I was settling down with a fat folder of clippings from magazines and newspapers entitled "Cee Gee Jones."

An hour later I went back to the librarian.

"I'd like the other file on Cee Gee Jones," I said.

He looked confused. "You have the file on Cee Gee Jones."

"No, I want the file on her years in Georgia. Before she came to New York."

"You are holding the only file we have. Remember when I helped you pull up the call number for Cee Gee Jones on the computer? There was only one file."

"But there must be another one. Either that or there are a lot of clippings missing from this one." I plunked it down on his desk.

"That's impossible." He picked it up and began shuffling through it. "You must have missed the material on the early years. I'm sure we'll be able to find what you're looking for . . ." He began to flip through the file. "I don't believe this."

"Something wrong?"

"There should be scads more than this. I mean tons. Just a minute."

He took off and returned minutes later with a formidable-looking woman many years his senior.

"There were at least twenty articles in this folder on Cee Gee's Jones's early career," she said after looking through it. "I know because I've been a clerk here for more than seventeen years and I clipped some of them."

"So what happened?" I asked.

"Someone must have taken them," she said grimly.

"Every once in a while it happens in spite of our best efforts," said the librarian. "But don't you worry, we'll find the vandal."

"How can you?" I asked.

"Remember you had to give me your name and your place of work on your requisition slip? And then you had to give me two forms of ID? We save those slips. It may take me a day or two, but eventually I'll trace the last person to take out that file. Since we haven't had any other complaints, it's most likely that whoever had it last took the clippings."

"Our system is most effective," said the clerk fervently. "We take a dim view of people stealing from the Billy Rose collection."

"Would you like me to notify you if we're able to recover the material?" asked the librarian.

"Please." I leaned in and whispered in his ear, "It's very important to . . . You Know Who."

I left him glowing with religious fervor, and headed east for my lunch with Freddie.

24

I like the Russian Tea Room. I know it's considered corny these days, but that's okay. It's always been corny. The original patrons were displaced Russian aristocrats and ballet dancers, for God's sake. The owners have spruced the place up in the last few years, painting over the old ballet murals in the process, which is a pity. But they still keep the elderly samovars scattered about, and the Christmas ornaments still stay on the art deco chandeliers year round. More important, the kitchen still serves the same blinis with caviar and sour cream that Freddie and I ordered when he took me there to celebrate my first job fifteen years ago. Of course, these days we both order a salad with dressing on the side—but I like knowing the blinis are still there.

I waited until after we'd been served our roughage; then I asked casually, "Freddie, what do you know about Cee Gee's early days?"

He frowned. "Why?"

"Just curious."

"You're involving yourself again, aren't you, Angie?" Freddie may hold a black belt in gossip himself, but he doesn't like it when I poke around in matters that he considers none of my business. He was horrified when I "involved" myself—his word—in the *Bright Tomorrow* murder.

"You're the one who always tells me I should know the people and the history before I begin a job," I said innocently. "I'm just following your advice."

Freddie loves it when I take his advice. But he didn't trust me. "You're sure you're not trying to get yourself in the middle of this Grace Shipley nightmare? Because believe me, *Liebchen,* no one in the business wants to hire a buttinsky who goes around yanking skeletons out of closets."

"Freddie, what happened on *Bright Tomorrow* was blind luck."

Coupled with a natural gift for detective work—but no need to mention that.

"I couldn't do it again if I wanted to. However, if you don't want to tell me the story, I'll just have to find someone who will. I'll bet Townie knows a tale or two . . ."

"You wouldn't."

"I'd be very tactful. Speaking of which, I don't think it's sensitive of you to refer to the tragic death of a woman cut down in her prime as 'this Grace Shipley nightmare.' "

At that point, Freddie requested that I please shut up so he could practice a couple of his stress-management techniques.

"Feeling better?" I asked after observing a moment of silence.

"Much. I just have to keep reminding myself that it's my own fault I'm in show business. Did I ever tell you about the time my mother got on her knees and begged me to become a podiatrist?"

"With great regularity. Freddie, all I want is a little information. Now, I know Cee Gee got her start at a small station in the South. And I know there was a story connected—something about a guest on her show—and I think it's all tied up with her daughter, but I don't know the specifics. I've read her autobiography, but she glosses over that time in a couple of sentences. It's kind of like, 'And then I had a talk show and I met Townie and I became a star.' And trust me, the book goes into loving detail on other periods of her life."

"Maybe she wants to forget about that part. And if she does, Angie, you as a loyal employee should forget it too."

"But why would she feel that way?"

"She took a certain amount of heat for what happened. Some people felt she exploited a crazy situation and made it a whole lot worse than it was just to get attention."

"So you do know the story."

"It's not exactly a secret."

"But I want your sense of nuance, your special insight . . ."

He hesitated for a few more beats, then finally said, "Oh, all right." Sometimes flattery will get you everywhere. And Freddie does love to dish.

"Cee Gee started in the early eighties," he began. "She was a hostess on a morning call-in talk show in Alabama—or Mississippi. Someplace like that."

"Actually, I think it was Georgia."

"Wherever." Freddie dismissed all of Dixie with the gesture of one who has his back issues of *New York* magazine bound and arranged chronologically on his bookshelves. "She had a daughter; however, at that point she was claiming to be a divorcée. Her show was popular—but it was in a small market and Cee Gee was ambitious. Townie came on as her producer, and they hit it off because they both wanted to get the hell out of whatever Squat Hollow they were in. But nothing was happening. Then they got lucky. One morning Cee Gee was on air interviewing a guest who was young, female, had an attitude problem and a kid without a daddy. The girl freely admitted that the short list of possible candidates for her child's paternity went into the double digits. Several of the more virtuous members of the viewing audience called in to attack her. She got upset, and started to cry. Which moved Cee Gee to deliver a spontaneous monologue on the healing power of compassion, understanding, forgiveness, and motherhood."

"It must have been something else."

"According to the Myth of Cee Gee, the station switchboard went bananas. Also according to the myth, that was the first time Cee Gee signed off by asking God to help her viewers be good to each other."

"Since then she's dropped God."

"These things happen. It's possible that He didn't test well in the focus groups after they got into the bigger markets."

"And they got into these markets because of one feel-good riff on a talk show? Cee Gee's good, but she ain't that good."

"Not so fast. Remember you said you wanted nuance."

I was beginning to be sorry about that.

"The excitement would have died out completely, but Cee Gee and Townie got another break. Someone starting making threatening phone calls to this girl. The police weren't much help—she wasn't exactly Miss Congeniality as far as they were concerned—so she went back to Cee Gee's show for help.

"Now, this is where people say Townie and Cee Gee exploited the situation. Because they used that girl and her problem to turn the show into a telephonic therapy group—they invited listeners to call in and share their feelings. Which gave Cee Gee an opportunity to continue doing those little think pieces on love and understanding."

"In other words they created the format they use today— minus a few refinements."

"And they started blowing away the competition on the other networks. Unfortunately, they also increased the local hostility against their guest. Someone took a couple of shots at her one morning as she was leaving her house."

"Don't tell me, let me guess. And Cee Gee told the story on air."

"And then she took the woman and her daughter into her own home. Putting herself at risk in order to protect them."

Okay, I gave her points for guts. But it would have been well worth it. I could just imagine the press releases. "At what point did Townie hire Cee Gee's first publicist?" I asked.

"I think it was after she hired the bodyguard."

"Ah yes. For the photographers."

"Well, they were starting to get national coverage."

"I'm sure."

"And that was when Cee Gee decided to come clean about her own daughter being illegitimate."

"Which she did on air because she realized she had to be honest about herself and communicate her pain so she could become a part of the healing process." And to hell with what it might do to Samantha someday.

"You don't need me to tell this story. You already know it."

"At this point it almost writes itself."

"The ratings went through the roof."

"And Townie recorded the show."

"No, Grace Shipley did that. She was the station manager."

"So that was her contribution."

"A big one as it turns out. The story had gotten enough attention in the press that several distributors were asking to see demo tapes of Cee Gee's work. I know a couple of people who claim to have seen bootlegs of that confession show and they say it was a real gut-wrencher."

"And after it was seen by the suits, we fast-forward to Cee Gee and Townie checking out studios for their new show in New York."

"It didn't go quite that fast, but yeah, basically that was the scenario."

"What happened to the guest?"

"I guess she stayed down in Squat Hollow."

"Did anyone from Cee Gee's organization stay in touch with her?"

"I doubt it."

"What was her name?"

"Who knows?"

Suddenly I wasn't hungry. I pushed my plate away.

"Something wrong with your salad?" Freddie was on the alert.

"It just occurred to me that my two-year contract could take a very long time to serve out."

"Angie, I cannot believe you're going judgmental on this. Are you or are you not the woman who once ran three concurrent stories on your soap opera about mothers and daughters who were having affairs with the same men?"

"Not my proudest moment, but at least that was fiction. Doesn't it bother you that this show exploits real life?"

"Fiction, real life—it's all television."

"Profound, Freddie."

"No, practical. Cee Gee and Townie needed a way to get noticed. An opportunity was handed to them and they made the most of it. The point is, once they got the attention, they delivered. Cee Gee's the best at what she does. We should all have her ratings."

"To say nothing of her bucks and clout."

"From your mouth to God's ear. Now Angela, enough bullshit." He leaned forward and looked at me the way he does when he's afraid I'll do something stupid and hurt myself. In his way, Freddie truly loves me.

"Repeat after me," he prompted sternly. "The difference between a pro and a talented amateur is . . ."

I pulled back my plate. He was right. "The pro doesn't have to be in love to do the job well," I recited.

"Good girl. Now eat your seventeen bucks' worth of front lawn."

We munched together in silence, while I thought about the story I'd just heard. I was looking for something in it that might scare three extremely successful and powerful women for many years. But there was nothing. Or if there was, I couldn't find it. I moved on to another area.

"Freddie, where did Grace Shipley fit in?"

"She was senior producer."

"I meant in the pecking order. What was her slot?"

"She didn't have one."

"But she was one of the most powerful people in the organization."

"Not really. That was always a little strange."

"In what way?"

"Let's say you were booking a client on *Cee Gee!*—for instance, a couple of years ago they did a show on the hot hunks of daytime and they used a kid of mine named Turk Ripper; don't laugh, he had a personal manager with zip taste—you had maybe one call with Grace Shipley. After that, you dealt with the show's producer or the associate producer. And if you had a serious problem you spoke with Townie, or even Felice, which was really strange since she's Cee Gee's personal assistant and technically doesn't have anything to do with the running of the show."

"But if Grace was senior producer, she should have been the troubleshooter."

"That is the job description."

"So why wasn't she?"

"The way I've heard it, as the show got bigger they knew Grace wasn't up to the job, so they gave her a title but they kept her out of the loop."

"Why not just get rid of her?"

"Loyalty. Cee Gee couldn't stand to fire her because they were old friends."

But I'd thought it was Townie who had protected Grace.

"They all go back a long time, don't they?"

"Been together about thirteen years. And now, thanks be to God, you are one of them. I propose a toast." He lifted his glass of the Italian—or possibly it was Belgian—water we'd ordered because Freddie wouldn't have been caught dead imbibing spirits in the middle of the day in this puritanical decade, and I'm not a drinker. I hate it when I find myself on the cutting edge of a trend.

25

My first thought when I got back to my apartment building was that the outsized stretch limo parked in front of it would never make it down the street. The city doesn't plow the snow in my neighborhood the way it does in those areas where the residents can afford vehicles the size of the *QE 2*. Then I wondered who the thing was waiting for. So when the door opened and the driver hopped out and began hailing someone, it didn't occur to me that he was after me. Until he called my name. But after he ushered me into the back seat, I understood everything.

John-Anne and Felice were in the car, sitting side by side. And just by seeing them together I knew my hunch about Felice's lover had been on the money. John-Anne had known about the doll in the bathroom because she'd learned about it through pillow talk with Felice. Damn, I love being right about this stuff.

John-Anne took Felice's hand protectively. "See if you can talk some sense into her," she said to me. "I've been screaming ever since I got your message on my machine."

"I assume you're Felice's alibi for Christmas Eve day."

"We were together from noon to about four-thirty. Our own little Yuletide/Kwanza celebration."

"The police should know that."

Felice looked nervously at the window separating us from the driver.

"He can't hear a thing," said John-Anne. "That's why we rented this damn car, remember?"

"I can't tell them," said Felice miserably. "You all just don't know what would happen. Townie doesn't like me anyway. And Carrie Gaye would never understand."

I looked to John-Anne for enlightenment.

"Carrie Gaye is Cee Gee's real name. Dates back to when she and Felice were little bitty girls going to Sunday school together," she said in a bad parody of a southern accent. It was a good thing she wasn't an actress, she had a lousy ear for dialects.

"Carrie Gaye's old-fashioned—like me." Felice was practically wailing. "She still reads her Bible every night."

"And if she's shocked by us after all the freaks she's interviewed on that show of hers, I want to meet the person who did her lobotomy," said John-Anne.

"Felice, I'm not sure you realize how serious this is," I said. "Do you know about the black fibers the police found in the doll's hair?"

She nodded miserably.

"Well, they asked me if you were wearing black on the night of the Christmas party and if you touched the doll."

"Me? But Grace did that mess with the doll."

"It may have been Grace, or it may not," I said, trying to project an aura of insider knowledge. "We . . . uh, the police have to consider every possibility."

"Are you saying they suspect Felice?" John-Anne was bristling. "What the hell for?"

"They suspect all of Cee Gee's nearest and dearest at this stage of the game," I said, and wondered if it was true. Well, it sounded good. "But Felice has put herself in an extremely vulnerable position because she's obviously lying about where she was at the time of the murder."

"Oh Lord," Felice moaned.

"Look, I promise you that Detective O'Hanlon will do everything she can to keep your private life out of the press."

"Right. She's done a great job of keeping things quiet so far," said John-Anne grimly.

I didn't have an answer for that one because it did seem to me that the media had an amazing amount of information on the murder. I flashed back to Patrick's comment that there were people in the department who were going to make sure Teresa couldn't control the case.

"But it doesn't matter about privacy anymore, hon," John-Anne said to Felice. "You and I are going to the police."

"Townie will fire me," said Felice. "Hell, I'd fire me too. Can you imagine how the fan clubs will take it—Cee Gee Jones's oldest friend and personal assistant is gay?"

"Her stylist is gay. So are most of the guys who escort her to her awards ceremonies."

"That's different and you know it."

John-Anne looked upward for strength. They'd been through this before. "So what's the worst they can do, fire you? Let them."

"I like making a living."

"You have more money than you'll ever need."

That won a sad chuckle from Felice. "Ain't no such thing as enough money for this ol' country gal, girlfriend." It seemed to be a joke between them.

"Felice has simple needs," John-Anne explained. "Money, jewelry, cars."

"And a nice little stock portfolio," added Felice. "Especially now that I get my advice from dear old George."

"George, as in George and Townie?" I asked. Which was a big mistake. Felice was looking for a way to change the subject.

"Bet you thought Townie supports him," she said eagerly. Next to her, John-Anne shifted impatiently, causing her corn-row beads to click together. "Felice . . ." she said.

"Everyone thinks that," Felice rushed on. " 'Cause George gave up his family business when Townie finally agreed to marry him. I think the poor fool thought they were going to go around the world together or something. But now he spends his time waiting on her to finish working, and—"

John-Anne tried again. "Felice . . ."

"The man is a natural-born gambler. 'Cause I don't care what anybody wants to say about Wall Street, it's nothing more than Las Vegas with class. I should know, my daddy was a gambling man. Only difference between him and old Georgie—Georgie's good. You ever fool around with the market, Angie?"

"I've never had the cash to lose."

"Neither do I. But that doesn't stop me."

"Felice!" John-Anne shouted so loud I was sure the driver must have heard it through the soundproof windows. Fortunately he didn't look up from the video game he was playing on his laptop computer.

Felice opened and closed her mouth a couple of times but no words came out. Her eyes started to fill with tears. "They've been my whole world for so long," she whispered finally.

"We're the most successful team in the business." The tears spilled over and ran down her ruddy cheeks. "I have my own table at The Grill." Then a long shuddery sigh. "I don't want Carrie Gaye to know."

"Damnit, you have nothing to be ashamed of." John-Anne's anger made her voice harsh. "If your breeder friends can't accept you for what you are, fuck 'em, and I do not mean that in the complimentary sense of the word. I know Cee Gee's been good to you. I've heard all about how if it wasn't for her you'd still be giving manicures in the front room of your dou-ble-wide. But this is murder we're talking about and your ass is on the line." Felice turned away. John-Anne patted her hand and continued more gently. "It'll be okay, hon. I'm with you. Anyway, it's time you came out to them. I've had it with sneak-ing around doing the Love That Dare Not Speak Its Name bullshit. These are the nineties."

For a moment the only sound in the car was that of Felice sniffing fiercely. Finally she turned to me.

"It all seems so unreal. I mean, I just can't believe that the police would think one of us killed Grace."

"I know," I said, remembering the first time I realized that everyone I knew and loved on *Bright Tomorrow* had suddenly become a potential suspect. "But someone did do it, Felice." I didn't add because I didn't have to "And it's more than likely that it was someone you've known for a long time."

Felice looked out the window of the car. "I hate these damn New York winters," she said. "Did you know there are flowers blooming in Georgia now? We call 'em rose of Sharon—Christmas roses."

John-Anne signaled to me to open the car door. As I started climbing out of the seat, she leaned over and said softly, "She'll be okay now. She needs some time, but she knows what she has to do. Thanks."

I nodded and exited from the car. It started up and I watched it maneuver smoothly down the street without getting stuck.

26

By the time I got back inside my apartment, it was after five.

Not that I needed a lot of time to get ready for my dinner date. I certainly wasn't planning to get dolled up for a glamour boy I'd decided was all wrong for me. But there was the dress. And the new sheer stockings with seams which I'd stopped to pick up on my way home from the library because somehow panty hose would be wrong with the dress. And the worth-its-weight-in-gold perfume Connie had given me for Christmas. And of course, I had to spend a bit of time rummaging through my lingerie. I have a thing for pretty lingerie—I'm partial to satin and French silk, any color except white, and lots of lace trim and ribbon rosettes. I finally settled on a tulip bra and lace panty set in a shade called "jewel-tone red," which matched the dress perfectly. Not that anyone was going to know that except me.

Then, for some reason, it didn't seem right to simply wash my hair and hope for the best the way I usually do. So I went to work with the blow dryer. And while I was at it, I hauled out the lip liner I seldom bother with. And the contouring blusher. And the three shades of taupe eye shadow.

When I was finished I spun around in front of my mirror feeling like Cinderella. Or Angie DaVito at fifteen all dressed up for her first Holy Angels/St. Michael's mixer. A thought which almost sent me back to the bedroom to change. But at that moment the doorbell rang.

I opened it and there was Patrick—dressed for an evening of bowling at a suburban shopping mall. No way you'd accuse him of being chic. Or even current. He'd had to hunt for those dated nondesigner jeans, that nondescript sweatshirt, those Top-Siders.

We stared at each other. Then just to add to the sitcom quality of the moment, we both said simultaneously, "I thought— " and stopped.

"You look terrific," he started again.

"So do you." He did, but that was because he would have looked terrific wearing anything. Or not. But I wasn't going to think about that.

"I thought the restaurant would be in the neighborhood," he said. "A family place that's been around for years." He was confused—clearly, he wasn't used to misreading the signals or the woman in a situation like this—but he didn't seem upset.

It disturbed me to realize that I was.

"I made a reservation at Stella."

"Why?" He was genuinely surprised.

"I thought you might like it."

"I do, but you won't."

"Why the hell not?"

"It's not your kind of place."

"How do you know what my kind of place is? What makes you think you know anything about me?"

Now he was getting upset. And mad. He did his jaw-tightening thing again. This time I caught it in profile. "Angie," he said too calmly, "if you want to go to Stella, it won't take me two minutes to go home and change clothes."

If he left I was going to burst into tears. Which really pissed me off.

"No, I'll change. We'll go to a place I know called Tony's." But I didn't want to change. I didn't want to lose that Cinderella feeling. Or the look of appreciation I'd seen in Patrick's eyes. Damnit.

Then he turned everything around by moving in and kissing me. He did it well. Too well, I tried to tell myself. But then I got busy kissing him back. So when the doorbell rang, it came as something of a shock.

Samantha came flying in. This time she was wearing dark glasses and a strawberry-blond wig which made her look jaundiced. She was carrying a Bloomingdale's shopping bag.

"I didn't want to take a chance on calling you from the apartment," she said breathlessly. "Everything's totally fucked and—" She stopped short at the sight of Patrick. "Oh wow," she said. "I didn't realize . . ."

"Samantha Jones, I'd like you to meet Patrick Gallagher. Patrick is the brother of my friend Detective O'Hanlon," I added.

The kid was nothing if not fast on the uptake. "Oh shit," she said.

27

Fortunately, Samantha seemed to be an old hand at tight situations.

"Angie, I'm so sorry to bother you," she said. She sent a tremulous little smile in Patrick's direction, then turned back to me.

"It's just that I heard something . . . It's about Robert . . . and I kind of freaked . . ."

"Oh yes," I said quickly. "Patrick, will you excuse us?"

"Of course," he said, with a smile that I found ominous.

"Okay, what about Robert?" I asked after I'd ushered Samantha into my bedroom and carefully closed the door.

"The scumbag is going on that show after all; Townie heard about it from some friends on the Coast. He's probably thinking look what the exposure did for Kato Kaelin's career. And after I bribed him, too—the son of a bitch. But forget him. I just had to find some way to get you away from Studly Do Right out there. Nice choice, by the way. Short, but then so are you. And that is a world-class butt."

"Samantha, if you barged into my apartment . . ."

"All hell is breaking loose, Angie. Mama doesn't have an alibi."

"Yes she does; at the time of the murder she was at the studio working on the promos for next season. There was an assistant with her who can vouch for her."

"That's not what Peggy says."

"Peggy Lawton?"

"She was the one who was with Mama. She went up to the third-floor editing room to work on one of the tapes. Then she brought it back down so Mama could look at it. Mama says she was gone for half an hour. At the most forty minutes. Peggy says she's sure it was longer."

"How much longer?"

"Over an hour."

Enough time for Cee Gee to have gone down the spiral staircase to her dressing room, through the second studio, and out the back entrance without anyone in the studio knowing it. Enough time for her to have gone crosstown to her apartment and back the same way. It would have been tight but she could have done it.

"When did Peggy say this?"

"Today. The first time she talked to the police, she agreed with Mama. But then today she said she'd lied because she wanted to be loyal to Mama and Townie because of everything they'd done for her, but she had to follow her fucking conscience. Townie fired her on the spot."

I bet she did. Talk about a lousy career move.

"Has anyone spoken to Peggy since all of this happened?"

"No, she's been making herself scarce. Townie told the guards at the studio to let her in so she could clear out her desk, but she never showed. All her stuff is still there." She shook her head.

"I always thought there was something weird about that chick. She kissed ass all the time, but I could never figure out why. I mean, with most of Mama's young hot shits you can tell what they want to be when they grow up. But Peggy didn't have an agenda. And there was something else strange about her. She never sucked up to me."

I remembered Peggy watching Samantha at the Christmas party. "Maybe she was jealous of you."

"No shit. The young ones all are. But they still try to make nice. They can't afford not to, I'm too important." She said it flatly, without rancor. "But whatever, Peggy screwed Mama good and that's why I want you to hide this crap for me."

She opened the shopping bag so I could see the familiar carton inside. "I thought we agreed the heart and the book should go to your mom's lawyers," I said.

"I was going to turn them over, but then the shit about Peggy went down. So I hid the box in the saddlebags on Mr. Alpert's bike down in the basement. He doesn't lock it in the storage room for the winter like everybody else because he wants people to know how butch he is, but he never uses it when the weather is cold so I knew—"

"Samantha, pay attention to me. The book and the heart are pieces of evidence in a murder investigation. You have to give them to the police."

"I can't. Not now." She was trying for her old defiance, but it came out as pleading. "Angie, if the cops arrest Mama you know what it will do to her career. No matter what happens later, people will always say there was something going on . . ."

"Who said anything about arresting Cee Gee?"

"Look at it: She knew about Al's gambling thing. She had two motives—me and the show. And now she has no alibi. That shit Grace sent her will make things look even worse."

She paused to swallow hard, "Mama's got millions sunk in that studio. I have to help."

"Samantha, your mother is a grown woman. You are a sixteen-year-old kid."

"Almost seventeen. But that doesn't matter. There isn't anyone else. You saw Townie—she's not handling this right, it's too real-life for her, and anyway, she's been running scared ever since the shit started with Grace. Someone's got to take care of business for Mama—cover her ass. You know how it is, Angie."

I did. Covering ass is an honorable profession in our industry. And Cee Gee Jones was one of those seductive types who seem to attract caretakers. Even her own daughter.

"Sammy, I'll make a deal with you. Let me give those things to Teresa and you and I will work together to see if we can figure out who did this."

She gave me a twisted little grin. "Angie and Sammy play Nancy Drew?"

I was already doing it. But it sounded so dumb when she said it out loud.

"You're right. Poor plan."

She was looking at me thoughtfully. "Maybe not. Nancy Drew kicked ass."

I held out my hand for the bag. She didn't give it to me. Instead she walked to the window and looked out. I don't have much of a view.

"What if . . ." she started, then stopped.

Somewhere out on the street, someone set off a car alarm. We could hear the tooting and hooting faintly through my locked window. Samantha drew a deep breath and tried again.

"What if we find out something . . . really bad, Angie?"

Given the circumstances, it was a distinct possibility. On the other hand, if *we* didn't, the police probably would.

"What are you afraid of?"

She turned. "It's just that Mama . . ." She trailed off.

"What about Mama?"

Silence. I decided one of us had to say it.

"Are you afraid your mother killed Grace, Sammy?"

"No!" The denial was vehement—maybe too vehement. "I know she didn't. No matter how mad Mama was, she would never . . . Well, she couldn't have." However, the anguish in her eyes said she'd thought a lot about the possibility that Mama could have. When Peggy Lawton changed her story she'd shaken Samantha badly. "I'm not talking about Mama— I mean, I don't think I am."

"Sammy, you're not making any sense. Just tell me what's bothering you."

"Are you going to tell the police if we find out something horrible while we're playing Nancy Drew?"

So that was it. "You're worried about whatever it was that happened down in Georgia, aren't you, Sammy? You're afraid it will finally come out."

She nodded. Outside the alarm cut off abruptly, midhoot. Either the owner had rescued the vehicle or there was a thief working the neighborhood who had a background in electronics.

"Honey, we may not discover anything. There may be nothing to discover. But I promise you—any secrets we can keep, we will. Okay?"

For a moment she looked at me. Then she picked up the bag and gave it to me.

"Where do we start?" she asked. She looked so young.

"Let's talk about Georgia. Do you know the name of the

guest who was on your mother's show? The one who moved into your house afterward?"

She looked puzzled. "I was only three years old when that happened."

"I know, but try to think."

She frowned with the effort to dredge up the past. "I remember her daughter. I hated the little bitch. She was older than me and she was really snotty about it. But I can't remember any names. I think it was one of those spooky southern jobs—something Mae something."

"Where did Ms. Something and her daughter go after they left your mother's house?"

"I don't know. It was a long time ago."

"And since then no one's ever mentioned them?"

"Well, I did ask Townie about them once. But she gave me a lecture about how the woman wanted to start a new life and we had to respect her privacy."

"But wasn't anyone even a little bit curious? After all, your mother was so concerned about them that she took them into her home."

"I don't think Mama gave a damn what happened to them. I think she hated that lady almost as much as I hated the kid."

Another piece of information. Which added nothing to my understanding of the matter.

"Sammy, will you do something for me? See if you can get the name of that woman from Townie or your mother."

A stubborn look crossed her face. "I can't do that. It'll fucking flip them out if they even know I was talking to you about this."

"I think we need that name."

She thought for a moment. "I could try calling the station down in Georgia," she said slowly. "It was in a town called

Macon. I think the woman came from somewhere around there."

In New York no one would remember after such a long time, but maybe in a small town . . .

"Give it a try," I said.

She looked at me warily. "You think this will help Mama?" she asked.

"I don't know what it will do. It's just a hunch."

She weighed it. "Okay," she said.

I sat on the bed and thought aloud. "So now we have to add Peggy into the mix—along with Grace and Townie and—"

"Angie, excuse me but aren't you forgetting someone?"

"If you mean Felice, I straightened out her alibi problem."

"I don't mean her. I'm referring to Mr. Gorgeous in the other room."

"Oh my, Patrick."

Sammy gave me a knowing look.

"You don't date much, do you," she said.

We rushed back into the living room, but Patrick was nowhere in sight. I told myself it didn't matter if he'd decided to leave. Samantha gave me another look.

Then we heard sounds coming from the kitchen. Samantha mouthed "Good luck" as she let herself out.

I strolled into the kitchen trying to look nonchalant. Despite the fact that I'd briefly forgotten the man's existence, I was awfully happy that he hadn't left. Sammy was right. There is a reason why I don't date more. She was also right about something else. That really was a world-class butt.

28

"Patrick, I'm sorry . . ." I began, but he was too busy contemplating the empty wasteland that was the interior of my refrigerator to pay attention. "Where's your food?" he asked.

"Do capers count as a vegetable?"

"No. Why do you have three jars of them?"

"I was going to make ratatouille once, but then I found out about all the chopping. Is there a reason why we're hanging out in the kitchen?"

"I thought since we missed your reservation at Stella maybe we could cook dinner. Something simple like an omelette."

"You need eggs for an omelette."

"Yes."

"I eat frozen food mostly. I don't suppose you'd go for some Weight Watchers zucchini lasagna?"

"Not really."

"I'll change and we can go to Tony's."

"Angie?"

"Yes."

"Does Teresa know about your meetings with Cee Gee Jones's daughter?"

Well, he was going to bring it up eventually. That was a given. Which did not make me any happier about it.

"I don't have meetings with sixteen-year-old children," I said.

"That 'child' is sixteen going on forty."

"Sammy and I talk."

"About the case?"

"Is that any of your business?"

"No, but it is Teresa's. Just don't make her job any more difficult than it already is, okay? Especially since you're the one who got her into this."

"Are you always this overbearing?" When feeling guilty, go on the attack.

"Me? Overbearing?"

"Allow me to rephrase. What does Teresa think of your smother-brother routine?"

"I do not smother!"

"You could have fooled me."

"You don't know what I do. You don't know me."

"No more than you know what kind of restaurants I like."

"Will you forget the damn restaurant?"

"No."

So he kissed me again. Which felt like a perfectly logical next step to me. And I would like to state for the record that he was one of those whose performance improves with practice. But then suddenly he pulled away.

"This is crazy," he muttered. "I don't usually . . ."

"What?" I demanded when I could get a breath. "Go for my type?" It was stupid how hurt I was when he didn't disagree. "Let me guess. It's actresses for you. Models with legs and zero brain function. Blondes."

"What I meant was—"

"You and Dudley Moore. What is it with short men?"

"If you must know," he shouted over me, "what I was going to say is, I don't usually go for the helpless type."

"Helpless? You're calling me helpless? I live alone in Manhattan. I produce television shows. I—"

"You fall down crossing streets, you eat Styrofoam food, you don't have anywhere to go on Christmas Eve, and—"

"Just what I need—a personality assessment from a man who calls himself Mother Maggie."

"And you fucked up our evening because of a tough little cookie who—"

But he had to put the rest of his thoughts on hold because the doorbell rang again and I had to answer it. This time it was the cops who appeared—specifically, a cop: Patrick's sister. Who waltzed in saying, "Angie, you really should do something about your doorman. He'll let anyone in the building without—" She stopped at the sight of her sibling and exclaimed, "Shortstuff, what are you doing here?"

Shortstuff made a little grinding sound with his perfect teeth.

29

It wasn't the nickname that sent me over the edge, it was hearing the terminally formal Teresa O'Hanlon employ one. That and the look on Patrick's face. I did what I always do when the situation calls for diplomacy and tact. I started to laugh.

Which made Teresa come perilously close to laughing. Which made Patrick head for the door.

"Patrick, don't leave. I'm sorry," Teresa called out.

"I'm going to get some food, so we can all eat."

"I'd love Chinese," I cooed.

"Fine," he said. "And while I'm gone you can tell Teresa all about your guest."

The look I gave him was intended to end his life. He responded with a saintly smile and left me alone with his sister the detective.

"Your guest?" she asked gently.

"Sit down and let me tell you a story."

So I filled her in. I told her about Sammy's vague feeling that there were problems of long standing between the women who ran the show. I reported on my thwarted research attempt, winding up with Sammy's take on Peggy Lawton.

I didn't produce the shopping bag.

When I finished, Teresa studied me with that look I never can read, although I don't think trust is its major component.

"All things considered, that was quite thorough. Patrick must have been persuasive," she remarked dryly.

I thought about denying that he'd had anything to do with my decision to tell the truth, and then I decided to hell with it. "He seemed to feel I owed you."

"When it comes to the women in his family, Patrick can be a little . . ."

"Overprotective?"

"He thinks he's very liberated."

We exchanged cautious half-smiles. Neither one of us was thrilled to be discussing my erstwhile date, her brother. Teresa got back to business fast.

"Angie, I'm going to level with you." She started to pace. "The department doesn't like this case. Someone is leaking information to the press—it may even be someone on my own squad. Potential witnesses are being paid for their stories, which taints their testimony. There's no way to stop it—the media is throwing money around and everyone wants to be on television."

And according to Patrick, there were people in the department determined to make this rough on her.

"On top of that, we have a crime scene which was not reported until hours after its discovery. There's pressure to make this thing go away as quickly as possible. And now with Peggy Lawton's testimony . . ."

"With Peggy Lawton's testimony, Cee Gee Jones has become your major suspect." I finished the thought.

"There is some feeling to that effect," she said carefully.

"But you don't share it."

"I'm not ready to make an arrest. It just doesn't feel right to me."

That was enough to persuade me.

"I think there's something you should see," I said.

"Good," she said. Which I chose not to translate as "I knew you had something more."

I went into the bedroom and brought back the shopping bag. Teresa examined the contents of the carton and asked who, how, where, and why questions which I answered as fully as I could.

"Now do I have everything?" she asked at last. "My sense is that I do—finally."

"That's it. Honest."

Her look was a poignant comment on my ideas about honesty. "Angie, I came here because I need a better sense of the people connected with that show."

"I don't know them very well."

"I'd say you've made some inroads. Ms. Rovere paid us a visit this afternoon and told us the truth concerning her whereabouts at the time of the murder. According to her, you were the one who convinced her to come forward. And then of course, there's Samantha." She gestured toward the shopping bag, which was on the floor at her feet. "You've obviously made a few friends." She looked a little weary. "Give me impressions. Intuitions. What drives these people? What do they want?"

I took a moment. "Townie's into power," I said slowly. "Felice wants money, and position . . ."

"And Ms. Jones?"

"That's tricky. Cee Gee's a performer. I guess I'd have to say her image is what's most important to her. And her own ability to keep on believing in it. Cee Gee wants to love herself. And I think, as much as she can care about someone else, she loves her daughter."

"What about Samantha?"

"She's a lonely kid who needs someone to talk to. She's worried about her mother."

"That's understandable."

"Should she be worried, Teresa?"

It was a question I had no business asking, and for a moment I thought Teresa was going to refuse to answer it. But then she looked down at the bag at her feet, and made a decision. "At this point it seems that Ms. Jones and her immediate associates had the strongest motive for committing the murder. If what Ms. Lawton is saying is true, Ms. Jones does not have an alibi. Both Ms. Rovere and Ms. Townsend-Stuart do. Now it's altogether possible that there is someone else who had a motive—maybe someone who has no involvement with Ms. Jones's show."

But I could tell from her tone that she didn't think so. And neither did the higher-ups in the department who were putting pressure on her to make this go away with a quick arrest.

"What's Townie's alibi?"

"At the time of the murder, Ms. Townsend-Stuart was at Pratesi Linens picking up the monogrammed sheets and towels she and her husband were giving Ms. Jones for Christmas. She stayed at Pratesi for at least forty-five minutes because there was a mix-up in her order. Someone claiming to be her husband had sent a messenger to pick it up the day before. When Ms. Townsend-Stuart called her husband at their home in Connecticut, he knew nothing about it. So she had to choose another present." She paused, then added in her best neutral-cop tone, "Ms. Jones knew when Ms. Townsend-Stuart would be going to Pratesi. And she knew what was in the order because she and Ms. Townsend-Stuart always discuss their Christmas presents in advance."

So, knowing that she wanted Townie out of the studio for at least an hour, Cee Gee could have called Pratesi the day before. She could have claimed to be George's secretary—or, in the deep voice she used so well, she might even have claimed to be George himself. She could have described the order exactly, and sent a messenger to pick it up. A harried clerk, busy with the last-minute Christmas rush, wouldn't have asked questions.

"Who hired the messenger?" I asked.

"It was charged to Ms. Jones's show."

Poor Sammy.

"Okay, let's say—just for the sake of argument—that it was Cee Gee who killed Grace. Why do it in her own apartment? Talk about incriminating yourself."

"The murder took place at the start of a long holiday weekend. The building would be on limited staff, and many of the other tenants would be out of town. Ms. Jones's daughter was supposed to be in the country with Ms. Rovere and the servants. At some point Ms. Jones planned to come back into the city and deal with the body—at least that's how the theory goes."

And a very logical and well-thought-out theory it was too. Obviously someone had spent considerable time and energy coming up with it.

As if to underscore that somber note, the air was suddenly filled by a scream which sounded like it came from a soul in agony. This was followed by sustained, earsplitting static. It seemed to be coming from the direction of my front door.

"What the hell . . . ?" I yelled.

"I think it's your apartment intercom," Teresa shouted back. "I told your doorman he must announce people before he lets them come into the building."

"But nobody's tried to use that thing since the Vietnam War."

"That's bad security," said Teresa as I raced to the intercom and began yelling, "Rosario, can you hear me?" at the doorman. It was while I was threatening him with physical pain if he didn't shut off the damn intercom that Patrick reappeared.

"Moo Shu Pork anyone?" he asked over the din.

The good news was that Teresa didn't try to make a tactful exit and let us get on with our ruined date. There are some situations you can't salvage and it gets awkward if anyone tries. Besides, at that point we were all starving.

The bad news was, I got plum sauce on the Donna Karan.

That night sleep was a long time in coming. When I closed my eyes I saw Townie, Goddess of Ice, who for some reason was afraid of Grace. And Peggy, whose conscience had kicked in just in time to screw up the alibi of an employer for whom she claimed to have undying devotion. And Felice, who loved expensive baubles and had a secret. And Cee Gee's guest from Georgia, about whom nobody, including the Lincoln Center Library for the Performing Arts seemed to have any information. And Teresa . . . and Sammy . . . and Patrick . . .

When I finally drifted off I dreamed about the Cee Gee doll. Which turned into a Samantha doll wearing a black nylon wig. Teresa wanted to examine it for clues but I threw it over my shoulder and carried it out of the room. I think someone was singing "*Vesti la Giubba*" in the background. But then, in my dreams someone is usually singing something.

30

The next morning I woke up feeling blah. I growled at StarsAnswrFone and dragged myself out of bed. While the coffeemaker gurgled, I waited for a call saying the day's work at the studio had been canceled. But it didn't come. Obviously a little spot of murder wasn't going to stop the troops at *Cee Gee*! Finally I called the service back and gave them the studio phone number in case anyone wanted to reach me there, and left the apartment.

During the night snow had fallen. Not the attractive Norman Rockwell kind of snow—this was the gray, gritty stuff that swirls around at your feet and makes your bones feel cold. It was my first day at my new studio. And even though I wouldn't officially start work until the new year, it felt like I was already on the job. What I couldn't decide was whether I felt happy about it or not.

Outside the studio it was a zoo. The police barricades were up and the press was out in force. So were the fans.

"I'm not getting into that mess," announced my driver, who insisted on dropping me a block away from the mob scene. New York cabbies are not the fearless warriors they used to be.

I made a dash for the front entrance of the studio, where a

harried cop was checking off names on a list. Fortunately someone had remembered to put mine on it.

In the lobby, just out of sight of the reporters, I saw Felice, Cee Gee, George, and Townie, who was a vision in white and beige. A debate seemed to be in progress.

"This is ridiculous, Victoria," George was saying in a low, angry voice. "There is no need for you to be here today."

"But we have to show the world that we're not afraid," said Cee Gee. "We have nothing to hide. We believe in the truth and—"

George cut her off without a glance. "Victoria?" he said to his wife. "Why don't you send everyone home and get out of here?"

"Because Cee Gee's right. We have to keep on going as if nothing is wrong." She said it calmly, but her eyes were glittery. And she was holding herself too straight. "I won't let everything I've worked for be ruined, George."

"Darling, please . . ."

"No one is going to stop me." Each word was clipped and precise. "Not even you, George."

For a moment they stood absolutely still, staring at each other. Then the tension seemed to go out of him. "All right, Townie," he said gently. It was the first time I'd heard him employ the nickname used by the rest of the world. I had a feeling it was deliberate. "I'll come back this evening to pick you up," he said. "I don't want you leaving this madhouse by yourself."

He turned and walked out of the building. Townie watched him battle his way through the crowd of reporters outside the studio, then turned to the rest of us. "Shall we go?" she asked briskly. And we marched down the fake marble hallway to the elevator.

On the second floor Townie took me to the main desk and introduced me to a sharp-eyed young woman named Sara who seemed to have taken Peggy Lawton's place as all-purpose handmaiden.

"Sara will take all your phone messages until next week when you actually start work. Then we'll set up E-mail, a fax, and voice mail for you." She favored me with a brittle smile before turning to Felice. "Show Angie around—she never did get a proper tour of this place. Then bring her to my office." And she bustled off.

"So you're still here," I murmured to Felice. "What did I tell you?"

"Townie has other fish to fry now. But she'll get to me in time." She looked out over the rabbit warren. "I love this place so much," she said.

I could see how much. And it made me wonder. Ostensibly, John-Anne was her alibi. But John-Anne wouldn't be the first lover or spouse to lie for a partner. If Grace had known about Felice's relationship with John-Anne and threatened to tell . . . The first time I met Felice I'd had the feeling she wouldn't shy away from a little physical violence to settle a dispute.

"Come on," she drawled. "I've got my orders; I'm supposed to show you around." Was it my imagination, or was her accent suddenly more pronounced? And weren't all southerners handy with guns?

The wild and woolly energy I'd seen before was gone from the second floor. Now the place resembled the waiting room outside an intensive care unit which catered to predominantly female clientele.

The weaker sex was represented by two cowed young men huddling together in a corner. They wore black silk shirts, black slacks and had identical chin stubble. Both looked distinctly unhappy.

Near them were two thirtyish Murphy Brown clones muttering to each other about the indignity of being fingerprinted. One young woman told another about her mother's reaction when the police came to the apartment to question her on Christmas Day.

My tour of the second floor was quick and dirty—this was not a day for lingering. Felice pointed out the large areas of office space which were given over to PR, financial, legal, and marketing departments. She raced me through the main conference room, where the staff held pitch sessions and production meetings. I was glad to see it was a large, comfortable mess. The staff lounge Joey had mentioned was luxurious and boasted a gym. There was a dining room in which breakfast and lunch were catered for the entire staff. As we whizzed past all this grandeur I tried to seem impressed—and tried not to think about how the hell I'd ever adapt.

Finally, once we'd circled the entire floor, we arrived at Cee Gee's office, Cee Gee was not to be found. "She must be with Townie," said Felice.

I saw the door that led to the downstairs dressing room. And another on the opposite side of the room.

"Does that go to Townie's office?" I asked. Felice nodded. "Is it kept locked?"

"Are you kidding? Townie and Cee Gee aren't big ones for privacy. They're always barging in on each other's meetings. They even cut in on each other's phone calls. They'd never lock that door."

In my mind I pictured another door, a small gray metal one, in the back of the building. It was labeled "Emergency Exit," but it was also an entrance. And it could be reached through the back route from Cee Gee's office. Or, I now gathered, from Townie's office, by way of Cee Gee's.

"Felice, who has the key to the back entrance? The one off the second soundstage?"

"Anyone who might need to bring a guest into the studio in secret. I have one; so do Cee Gee and Townie and Grace—well, now I guess you will, and the office assistant, although now that Peggy's gone we don't have a new one yet—and any of the producers. Why do you ask?"

"Just trying to acclimate myself. Where's my office?"

"You'll be taking Grace's . . . I'm afraid we haven't had time to pack up her things."

"No problem, I'm not picky about my surroundings."

She nodded and led me back out into the hallway.

"Grace's office—that is, my office—doesn't connect to the other two?" I asked.

"No. Townie and Cee Gee didn't think it was necessary. The phones were enough."

Further evidence, it seemed to me, of just how far Grace had been out of the loop.

We stopped before a door and Felice ushered me inside. "Here it is," she said—and then added quickly as she saw the look on my face, "Of course, you'll probably want to redecorate."

I nodded wordlessly. Because Grace Shipley had embraced the powerful-woman-in-television decorating mode with a vengeance. An explosion of cabbage roses had occurred in this room. The stench of potpourri still lingered. Anything that was not swagged or draped was pleated or ruffled. Mounds of puffy pillows covered the chairs, the sofas, and a boudoir-size chaise longue.

"Where do I sit?" I asked.

"I'll tell the maintenance people to strip the place," said Felice.

After which they could fumigate it.

"Thank you."

"Townie's office is next to yours. As soon as you're ready, check in with her."

And Felice left me alone in Grace's flower bower. I tried opening a window, but they were all sealed shut. I tried yanking back the curtains to let in a little daylight, but they were cleverly weighted for maximum immobility. I was thinking wistfully about blowtorches and firebombs when the phone rang. I dove for it.

"It's a Mr. Gallagher, Angie," said Sara at the switchboard.

"About that dinner . . ." said Patrick, who had the slightly fuzzy quality of one who had not been awake long. I liked the way he sounded when he was half asleep. I'd probably like the way he looked and smelled, too, if I were cuddled up next to him . . . Which I wasn't, I reminded myself.

"Want to try again?" he asked. "You pick the restaurant and I promise there will be no commentary."

It was absolutely ridiculous for me to be so pleased.

"Actually, I've been thinking about that omelette you offered to make," I said.

So we settled on seven o'clock at my apartment.

As soon as I hung up, I reported to Townie. The day was looking up.

31

For the rest of the morning I hung out with Townie, getting a crash course in both talk television and mental discipline. The way the woman was able to block out all distractions—including the press, which continued to circle the building—was amazing.

Townie treated her team of young producers like the front-line troops in a war zone—with hot guests and ratings being the spoils. They were savvy kids: aggressive, competitive, and almost as well disciplined as their leader. Each seemed to have a specialty. One of the Murphy Brown clones handled the celebrity shows. A gloomy young woman named Melanie worked on what were called the "relationship pieces." And they all came to Townie to solve their problems.

Melanie kicked off the morning with her concern about a family that had gone into therapy after being booked for a show entitled "When Your Loved Ones Hate Your Guts."

"I've talked to all of them on the phone and they say that goddamn shrink is teaching them to understand each other," she fumed. Townie helped her come up with a strategy to combat this potential disaster by sending several of the associate producers to the green room to agitate individual family members as they waited to tape the show. The APs, who had done this kind of thing often, knew exactly which emotional buttons to push. However, just to be sure, Townie promised her distraught lieutenant that they'd have a dry run the night before the show. With any luck, the clan would be at each other's throats by airtime. No sooner had Melanie expressed her thanks and withdrawn than three more of Townie's people came before her with similar problems.

And so it went. Townie listened to reports on shows in progress and held postmortems on shows that had already been completed. All morning long, I kept waiting for someone to say something about Grace Shipley. But no one even mentioned her name. Not once. By lunchtime I was beginning to wonder if I'd imagined her murder.

The silence finally broke that afternoon during the pitch session in the conference room. This was an informal meeting billed as a "discussion" of possible topics for future *Cee Gee* shows. Actually, "battle to the death" would have been a more accurate description as Townie's young sharks vied for airtime for their ideas. During one of the few calm moments, one of the young men sought and got the floor. "Why not capitalize on our own problem?" he suggested. "Let's address the issue of Grace Shipley before anyone else does."

There was a collective intake of breath in the room as the unmentionable was mentioned. Townie went very still.

"Here's the slant," the doomed young man continued. "We approach it as a story of history repeating itself. Draw a parallel between the things Grace did to Cee Gee and the time years ago when one of Cee Gee's guests was harassed."

"No," said Townie.

"But that was a very dramatic story," protested the fellow who obviously had a big death wish.

"You fool, I said no!"

"What Townie means—" Cee Gee began, but she was cut off.

"What Townie means is, we are not going to dredge up the past," Townie broke in. "No one cares anymore. Only an idiot would think it was of any interest today. I—" She stopped abruptly. "I will not dignify this kind of stupidity with the courtesy of consideration," she said, and walked out.

So much for mental discipline, I thought.

By five o'clock everyone but Townie was starting to fade. At six, while everyone else was eyeing the exit, she left her office and began wandering around the floor looking for more problems to solve. It was as if she didn't want the workday to end. Normally I take pride in being the last one to leave. But that evening I wanted to get out. And not just because of Patrick. I wondered what the protocol was for calling it quits. Was it like having dinner with royalty—did we have to wait until the Queen left the table?

At six-fifteen I decided to take matters into my own hands. I went to the front desk. "Any messages for me?" I asked a little too loudly. "Might as well take care of them before I pack it in for the day." If no one challenged me, I figured, I'd take off.

Unfortunately, it wasn't going to be that simple. When I approached Sara's desk I could see she was bursting with curiosity.

"You had two calls," she said eagerly. "One was from somebody who said he was a librarian at Lincoln Center. He said to please call him because he had some information about that research you were doing on the show. He left his number." She handed it to me, then paused mightily. Her sense of dramatic pace was excellent. "The other person wouldn't leave her name, but I thought it sounded a lot like Ms. Jones's daughter, Samantha. She calls here sometimes for her mother and the voice was awfully familiar." She looked at me with the kind of naked curiosity that demands a response.

"Dear Sammy," I said airily. "She's such a . . . sweet kid. I talked to her at Cee Gee's Christmas party and I told her I have a niece who lives near Cee Gee's home in Kent. I thought maybe Sammy and Maria Lucia could get together sometime when Sammy's in the country." It was a meeting that would take place over Connie's dead body, but what the hell. "I guess I should give the child a buzz. Did Sammy leave a number?"

Sara gave it to me. "You can use the phone here," she offered hopefully.

"Thanks, I'll go back to my office."

First I decided to take a shot that the librarian might still be at his desk. Luck was with me.

"You caught me just as I was leaving," he said. "There's something you should know about those clippings you wanted. You remember? The ones that are missing from the Cee Gee Jones file?" he asked in the kindly manner of Mr. Rogers dealing with the neighborhood.

Get on with it, I wanted to scream. "Right. The information on Cee Gee's career before she came to New York" was what I said.

"Well, the last person to take out that file did so one week ago. We haven't contacted her yet, but I thought you might be able to."

"Why me?"

"Because according to the information on her requisition slip she's a colleague of yours. You both work for Cee Gee."

My heart started beating faster. "Who is she?"

"I really shouldn't give out this information," he said coyly. He was lucky we were talking on the phone. If we'd been in the same room, I'd have hurt him. "However, since you probably know each other . . . Her name is Peggy Lawton."

"Are you sure?"

"The information was on her requisition slip," said he in the tone of one quoting Holy Writ. "Don't you know her?"

"Yes, I do. Thank you," I said, and hung up. But obviously I didn't know the first thing about the terminally cheery Ms. Lawton. So who did? There must be someone at this office who'd shared a coffee or a cab with her. Someone who would have some insights about the girl. But I didn't have time to find that person unless I wanted to be late for Patrick. So instead, I dialed Teresa at the station.

She wasn't at her desk. Feeling frustrated, I left a message telling her to get in touch with me at home.

Samantha wasn't available either. I resisted the impulse to slam down the receiver. Sammy had her own phone and she'd given me the number, but with one thing and another it seemed wiser not to leave a detailed message on her voice mail. I just stated my name and the time and hung up.

The phone calls had taken a lot of precious time, so I made a mad dash down to the lobby. Through the front windows I could see that the press was still outside in force, freezing its collective buns off.

"Damn," I said.

"Filthy creatures, aren't they?" said a voice at my side.

George, who had been waiting for Townie, came over to join me in watching them. "What kind of human being spends his days invading the personal lives of others—feeding off their tragedies and weaknesses?"

It was a question some people had been moved to ask of his wife.

"Forgive me for ranting, Angela of Life. You seem upset. May I help?"

"I'm afraid not. It's just that I'm already late, and getting a cab with that horde in place is going to be impossible."

"Then you must allow me to drive you to your destination. I have the van parked behind the studio and Victoria won't be ready to leave for another half hour at the earliest."

Since I had the feeling he was dying to get out of there, and I had twenty-five minutes before Patrick was due to appear on my doorstep, I accepted.

"I brought the van in from the country because those vultures from the fourth estate are looking for a Rolls or a limo," George said after we had successfully faked out the reporters and were tooling up Tenth Avenue. "Not only are they repulsive, they seem to be remarkably stupid."

I looked at him sitting next to me, erect and dignified. They don't make ramrod spines like that anymore. "You must dislike all of this very much," I said gently.

He sighed. "Particularly for my wife. It will sound foolish to you, I know, but I can still remember the days when a gentlewoman had her name in the newspapers on three occasions only—when she was born, married, and died." He turned and smiled his charming smile at me. "I'm quite an old fossil, you see."

"After today, I'm on your side all the way."

"Marvelous. We'll mount a counter-revolution. The escutcheon on our banner will be a lion crushing a television."

It was an interesting image for a man whose wife was one of the more important people in the medium. He seemed to pick up on what I was thinking.

"How was Victoria today, Angie?" he asked quietly.

"She's upset. Everyone is."

"Poor baby." He was lost in his thoughts for a moment. "Did you know she wanted to sing opera once? She had a sweet voice. Small but quite beautiful." His face went gentle, then sad with memory. "But she couldn't do it. She choked up with stage fright at her first recital. Literally couldn't make a sound. It was the first time she'd ever failed at anything. I've always felt that was why the show with Cee Gee had to be such a big success."

He got me to my building with ten minutes to spare. Then he insisted on parking and escorting me in. He waited while I informed Rosario that I was expecting a guest, walked me through the lobby, and kissed my hand in front of the elevator. He was probably one of four men still living who could have gotten away with it. I could feel how impressed Rosario was—my image in the building had just gone up a hundred percent. Which could come in handy the next time the toilet backed up.

32

"Angie, stop," said Patrick.

"I'm helping."

"You're going to cut off a finger."

"Nah, it just looks that way."

So then he had to take the knife away from me. Which meant leaving the stove and coming over—which was what I'd had in mind all along.

We'd started out being careful with each other. Patrick had shown up with elephant garlic, extra-virgin olive oil, and four kinds of mushrooms. I didn't make a single crack about trendy foodstuffs. In return he didn't even mention my lack of basic cooking utensils. He also produced a loaf of Mother Maggie's black olive bread, and her famous walnut–sour cream apple pie. I was properly appreciative. He was properly gracious. And I could feel both of us getting bored simultaneously. So we reverted to snappy patter and trying to bait each other, a habit we both seemed to enjoy.

"There's just something so sexy about watching a guy slaving over a hot stove," I sighed. "Sure you wouldn't like to put on an apron for me?"

So then naturally he had to show me sexy. Which was a lot more fun than watching him braise the garlic—or whatever the hell he'd been doing to it.

The evening was starting to turn into one of those you remember, when we were interrupted by a shriek from the intercom.

I grabbed it and yelled, "Rosario, if you ever use this thing again I will kill you."

"Angie, don't say that," Patrick protested over the static. "You have to have a security system."

"What is it with you and Teresa? Rosario," I screamed into the intercom, "I'm coming downstairs to maim you." At last, the thing went blessedly silent. "We have a perfectly lovely security system," I informed Patrick crossly. "Rosario kicks out anyone he doesn't recognize unless we warn him not to. If a guest arrives unexpectedly, they call from the street. Or they go home. It's simple. And it's quiet." The doorbell rang. "Your sister has a lot to answer for," I said as I opened it.

"My sister is absolutely right," said Patrick—as Teresa walked into the apartment.

We did one of those three-way looks that are never as funny in real life as they are on the stage.

"Patrick," said Teresa to him.

"You did this deliberately," said Patrick to me.

"I didn't know anything about it," I said to him.

"Hank said you called, Angie," said Teresa.

"You're getting back at me for last night," said Patrick, still to me.

"I left a message," I argued. "Be fair. Who knew this would happen? I expected a phone call not a house call."

"Hank thought you sounded urgent," said Teresa. "Besides, I prefer talking to you when I can see your face."

"I can certainly understand why," said Patrick.

"I resent that," I said.

"Patrick, is something burning?" asked Teresa.

I sniffed. "I think it's the garlic." Then as Patrick raced to the kitchen to attempt a rescue, I added virtuously, "I believe the first rule of all really fine cooks is to pay attention to what you're doing." I was rewarded with a mighty crash from the kitchen.

Then the doorbell rang again. With no warning from the intercom—a good sign which seemed to indicate that Rosarie had taken me at my word and abandoned the damn thing. Unfortunately, this was one time when I would have liked a little advance warning. Because Samantha burst in.

"Angie, I got the name. It's Margaret Mae Mapes. You won't believe how I—" As she had with Patrick, she stopped short at the sight of Teresa. But this time she didn't need an introduction.

"Good evening, Samantha," said Teresa.

33

"Gee Angie," said Samantha sweetly, "you didn't tell me your friend the detective was going to be here."

"I didn't know *you* were going to be here," I pointed out. I didn't add that I hadn't been expecting Teresa, either.

"How do you know about Margaret Mae Mapes, Samantha?" asked Teresa.

"Really, Detective O'Hanlon, I don't know anything much." Samantha gave her what was meant to be an artless schoolgirl smile. Since she'd probably never met, much less been, one, the performance wasn't half bad. Although something about it was familiar.

"How did you know the name?" asked Teresa.

"Well, it just popped into my head," she said. I noticed that somehow she'd gotten the blushing problem under control. "See, this lady, Margaret Mae Mapes? She was a guest on Mama's show a long, long time ago. And I told Angie that I couldn't remember her name and then all of a sudden it just came to me."

"So you came over here to tell Angie?"

"Well, yes. That, and I really wanted to get out of the apartment." She executed a nauseatingly cute little giggle, and I placed her act. She was doing Sally Fields in her Gidget period.

Teresa realized that she was getting nowhere. "Samantha,

let's sit down and talk," she said. She led her to the sofa in my living room. I was torn between a desire to follow them and see who would win, and other desires which had to do with the guy who was in my kitchen trying to make the smoke vent work. He solved the problem by sidling up to me and whispering in my ear, "When you finally get around to eating, remember that the bread tastes better if it's warm, but I wouldn't risk your broiler. And whatever you do, don't let Teresa make the coffee." He was wearing his coat.

"Where are you going?" I asked.

"Away."

"I'll get rid of them."

"Angie, take a good look at the woman in your living room. That is a Gallagher cop working on a case. Now let me tell you some family history. When he was walking the beat, my old man always pulled a straight eight—which is cop talk for he never even sat down, much less took a cup of free coffee for his entire shift. My grandfather was famous for getting his confessions by staying on his feet during an interrogation until he'd outlasted not only the perp but the entire precinct."

"And this has bearing on my present situation how?"

"Tunnel vision and stamina are programmed into my sister's DNA. Nothing you can say or do will budge her. And since I think that kid is also tough as nails, I'd say you have guests. So enjoy. You know you're dying to get in on the fun."

He was right, but not completely. Lust was still battling with curiosity. "You and I were having fun," I said.

"You and I are taking a raincheck," he said, which seemed to hold out some promise for the future, although I wasn't totally reassured. But then I'm never totally reassured when it comes to men.

"I'm sorry about this," I said.

"Hey, it's my sister." He gave me a chaste peck on the cheek and left.

"I think you're smart," Teresa was saying to Samantha when I returned to the living room. "And very observant. That's why I know you can help me."

"Boy, I sure don't see how, Detective."

Teresa realized she still wasn't getting anywhere and tried another approach. "Samantha, wouldn't you like to see this murder solved so everyone could get on with their lives?"

"Oh yes," chirped Sammy.

"Then will you trust me?"

Of course, that was the problem. It's very hard to trust when you're trying to protect someone else. And when you're trying to hide a murky secret, the specifics of which even you are not sure about. Sammy threw a quick look in my direction and I tried to convey "Tell Teresa the truth," but either she didn't get it or she decided to ignore it. She turned back to Teresa. "If you think I can help you, Detective, I'll do my best," she said, segueing into the more mature Sally Fields of Oscar-winning fame. "Plucky" was now the way to describe our gal Sam. "What do you want to know?" she asked.

"Let's get back to Margaret Mae Mapes," said Teresa.

"Isn't it funny the way you just think and think and think about something and then all of a sudden there it is?"

"So you're saying that you just happened to remember that name?"

"Well, I thought about it a lot."

"You must have been how old—two—when Margaret Mae Mapes was a guest on your mother's show?"

"Actually I was three. But I heard the name all the time. She was a very big part of our life."

It went on like that for about another twenty minutes. Finally Samantha announced with a virtuous smile that she had to get home to make her curfew. Teresa did not detain her.

"I wish I knew how that child came up with the name Margaret Mae Mapes," said Teresa after she'd gone. I did too. I still felt that somehow the elusive Ms. Mapes held the key to the riddle of Grace Shipley's death—not that I could do much about it at that moment. I suggested that we retire to the kitchen, where we were soon eating the best apple pie in the world. I thought regretfully of Patrick. His sister seemed oblivious. "It took us the better part of a day to track that name," she said, still following her own train of thought.

"So you came up with it too?"

"Of course—after I got your tip last night."

"What else did you find out about Margaret Mae Mapes? What happened to her?"

"She seems to have left the area shortly after her last appearance on the talk show."

"Where is she now?" I asked, trying to sound casual. My tone didn't fool Teresa for a minute.

"Angie, there really isn't a great deal of enthusiasm for this line of inquiry," she said. "I'm working on it, but the general feeling is that I'm wasting my time."

"Do you think you are?"

She mashed a few pie crumbs with her fork. "I think you'd better tell me why you called me," she said.

There was no point in trying to push her for more; history had taught me that there was no way you got anything out of

Teresa that she didn't feel like giving. So I told her about Peggy Lawton and the clippings.

"What's your assessment of Ms. Lawton?" Teresa asked when I'd finished.

I thought about Peggy. I remembered the way Joey and his gaffer had reacted to her. And I thought about all the things Samantha had said. "Peggy just doesn't ring true somehow."

"You mean she's a liar?"

"Not exactly. She's just one of those people other people don't trust. Peggy could be absolutely right about something and no one would believe her."

34

After Teresa left, I called Samantha's phone and got her voice mail again. This time I risked a message. "Sammy, I need the rest of it," I said, hoping that would mystify anyone else who might pick it up, while at the same time communicating to Sammy that I wanted to know who had given her Margaret Mae Mapes's name.

I thought about going to bed, but I couldn't get Peggy Lawton out of my mind. I wondered what spin she would put on the theft of the clippings if she was confronted about it.

It was late for me to be calling her—but that might throw her off balance a little, which would be good. Since I now had a *Cee Gee!* company roster, I looked up Lawton's number and dialed. There was no answer. And no answering machine or service, which was unheard of for a fast-track kid hoping for a career in television. The sacred eleventh commandment of the industry is: Thou Shalt Never Be Out of Touch. What the hell was going on with that girl?

I pictured her on the night of the Christmas party: frazzled, but still perky in her white lace dress. She'd watched Samantha flirting. Then she'd brushed off the cute young guy who did the audience warm-up. David something. I checked my roster: David Miller. I wondered what it had been before his agent convinced him to change it. David might have some thoughts about Peggy. Obviously he'd known her well enough to make a play for her. He wasn't on the production staff, so he wouldn't be coming into work until next week. But he did have to eat, didn't he? So how would he react if his new senior producer–to–be were to call him at this advanced hour and ask him to have lunch tomorrow?

David was out, but there was a message on his machine. "Hi, this is Dave," it said over a background of what sounded like the end of the world but was probably some new music group. "You know the drill, so do your thing after the beep. If you want to catch me doing mine, I'll be on for the midnight show at the Three S Club—that's Seventy-seventh Street Comedy Club, so get your mind out of the gutter, ha, ha. I'm on every night this week, except New Year's Eve—they get a real comedian for that. Bah dum bah. Seriously, come see me. I'm worth it."

It was a quarter to eleven. I still had time to get to the club and watch David do his thing, if I wanted to. There were several excellent reasons why I didn't. The most important of which was that David was going to be lousy. I knew this because small comedy clubs don't put on the good acts at midnight. They book the funny folk at nine o'clock when audiences are awake.

There were other reasons for minding my own business and going to bed. I was tired. I had to rise at the crack of dawn the next day. And this whole thing was probably a wild-goose chase.

I got my coat.

The posters outside the Three S Club advertised it as a handsomely appointed space. From what I could tell, this meant that the black velours backing the tiny stage were not too badly tattered, and the lighting didn't make the comedians look like they were dead. Just dying. Bah dum bah.

David's act was everything I'd expected it would be. I watched him work the six-person crowd and hoped that somewhere in his background there was a family-owned business—say a hardware store—that he could go into someday. He wasn't going to stay cute enough to charm *Cee Gee!* audiences forever. And Robin Williams he wasn't.

He came off the stage—at long last—and joined me at my table for a beer. Naturally the first words out of his mouth were, "What did you think?"

Not that he wanted to know. Not really. No performer does—forget the bull about constructive criticism. What he wanted was foot-stomping, hand-blistering applause. Which put me in a bind well known to those of us who work in show biz: What do you say to an acquaintance who has just bombed?

There are certain time-honored gambits. The most famous is to look the perpetrator of your awful evening squarely in the eye and say, "Love the suit."

Instead I tried an evasive "That was something else." But it didn't get me off the hook.

"But what did you *really* think?" he asked.

So I said, "Fabulous, David." Let his mother tell him the facts of life.

"Honest? You're not just saying that?"

"I couldn't believe it." Which was getting into the realm of truth. "I'm so glad I took a chance and came to see your act. I think we can work some of your own material into your *Cee Gee!* warm-up." God forbid. "Now tell me, have any of your friends from the show been here?"

"Well, I've been kind of holding off—to work out the kinks. Do you think I'm ready?"

"As you'll ever be." That, at least, came from the heart. "In fact, why don't I arrange for a little group to come one night? You'll want your girlfriend, of course."

"Which one?" He was being sincere.

"That sweet thing—what's her name? Peggy. Peggy Lawton."

An uneasy look crossed his face. "Peggy? She's not my . . . Jeez, whatever gave you that idea?" He unleashed a peal of fake laughter. "I mean . . . well, she's not even my friend. I hardly know her."

"Oh my, how silly of me. It's just that I saw you with her at Cee Gee's Christmas party and I thought . . ."

The look got uneasier. "Look, we just came crosstown from the studio together, that's all. 'Cause I felt sorry for her. She killed herself working at the apartment all day. Then she came running back to the studio to change and she had to get back over there and she couldn't get a ride. . . . I mean, there she was in that stupid white dress lugging that heavy garment bag. So I offered to share my cab with her."

Peggy was lugging the garment bag? I pictured her when she left the party. She was wearing jeans, a T-shirt, and sneakers. Not an outfit you'd have to lug, I'd have thought. And now that I thought about it, why had she taken such a big piece of luggage for such a small load?

"Exactly how heavy was the bag, David?"

"How would I know? She wouldn't let me near it. You've got to understand, we do not have a close relationship. Or any relationship."

"Do you remember what color the bag was?"

"Black, I think."

That was what I thought. I stood up and threw some money on the table. "David, it's been super, but I've got to run," I said.

"About that group . . ."

"Just get me a list of everyone you want."

"You think I should invite Townie and Cee Gee?"

"Uh . . . why don't you wait until the club puts you on at nine o'clock?"

Since that would happen at the time of the Last Judgment, it seemed like a safe suggestion.

Teresa was one of those loathsome people who wake up instantly and are fully alert when you call them at two o'clock in the morning.

"I want to know how it comes out," I said after I gave her the information.

"I've already told you too much."

"Teresa, I just sat through a twenty-minute comedy routine on bodily functions I normally refuse to think about."

It only took her a second. "I'll be in touch," she said. The woman is fair-minded.

I tumbled into bed exhausted. But just as I was drifting off it occurred to me that in my excitement about the garment bag I had overlooked something that might have been important. David had been uncomfortable with the suggestion that he and Peggy Lawton were close. In fact, he'd gone out of his way to distance himself from her. What was that about?

I forced myself upright and called StarsAnswrFone.

"After you wake me up this morning, say, 'Phone David,' " I instructed the bewildered operator. "Say it twice. Then call back fifteen minutes later to see if I've done it. Keep nagging me until I swear on my pension fund that the call has been made."

I fell back on the pillows secure in the knowledge I would remember to phone David Miller. StarsAnswrFone workers may not be great original thinkers, but they are rocklike in their ability to follow orders.

35

Teresa is a woman of her word. At ten the next morning she knocked on the door of my office at the studio. I turned to the bouncy little audience coordinator who was briefing me on the gentle art of stacking the house with fans when the guest was a celebrity. "Cindy," I said, "could I have a moment with Detective O'Hanlon?" Cindy's eyes grew big and she nodded. News of my relationship with the police would be all over the studio in the next fifteen seconds.

"Was I right?" I asked Teresa after Cindy had gone.

"I don't know yet. Based on the information you gave me, we're going to try to get a warrant to search Ms. Lawton's apartment."

"But what did Peggy say when you asked her?"

"We haven't been able to find her. She wasn't at her home this morning. That's why we came to the studio."

"She isn't here. She hasn't been back since she was fired. What are you hoping to find?"

"We want to check out a few things."

"Like what?" I was being pushy, but she owed me.

"Have a nice day, Angie," she said as she walked out. Well, if that was the way she wanted it . . . I waited until she'd been gone about five minutes before I went out into the corridor.

After making sure there were no cops in sight, I headed for the maze of cubicles.

David had not answered the phone when I called him that morning. I'd left a message with my number at the studio but he hadn't gotten back to me. So it was time to go hunting.

In every studio I've ever had contact with, there is always a grapevine. In my opinion, using it effectively is the mark of a good boss. The trick is to know where and to whom to leak information.

I found what I was looking for near the reception area. Cindy and Sara were engaged in a deep conversation which stopped too quickly when I approached.

"Do either of you know if David Miller might be coming in today?" I asked. "I was talking with Detective . . . that is, a friend of mine . . . and . . . well, forget it. It's not important," I said, frowning heavily to show that it really was, and stalked back to my office to wait. If David was home, I gave him fifteen minutes—twenty at the most—to get back to me. Meanwhile I entertained myself by spraying the room with air freshener and trying to cram the damn pillows into the two garbage bags I'd brought from home. Felice still hadn't had the place stripped.

David called on schedule and suggested that we meet at a coffee shop near the studio. There's nothing like a little bit of good old-fashioned manipulation and deceit, I always say.

I put in another call to Samantha, who either wasn't home or wasn't answering, and left a message telling her where I would be and asking her to meet me if she picked up anytime within the hour. Then I snuck out the back entrance of the studio.

———

"Okay, I lied a little about Peggy." David was slumped in the booth seat across the table from me. He looked tired and sulky—which cut his cuteness quotient by at least half. He'd have to watch that.

"Guys are an endangered species on *Cee Gee!*" he continued. "Especially straight guys who are . . ."

"Attractive."

He perked up considerably. "Well, whatever," he said modestly. "The thing is, I didn't know what kind of a nutcase Peggy was. And after I found out, I didn't want people thinking we were . . . you know, together or anything."

"In what way is Peggy a nutcase?"

He looked uncomfortable. "Long story," he muttered.

"I'm here to listen."

"Okay, this is what happened. The night of the party, after everybody left, I took her out for a drink to this place I know called Bright Lights. It was sort of stupid. Because normally I wouldn't have, she's not that pretty. But she'd dusted me off earlier and . . ." He flashed a grin that was supposed to melt me. "And frankly, that doesn't happen very often."

"So you were interested."

His shrug said, "Boys will be boys." Which is why I prefer men.

"I thought maybe a few drinks would loosen her up, but I never would have gone near her if I'd realized what a flake she is. I mean, that girl needs help."

"What happened?"

"Well, first she got blitzed. Which may have been my fault because I was egging her on. Then she started laughing and saying that we were both a couple of frauds because we worked for a con artist and our show was based on a scam. I tried to make her cool it, but that just turned her mean. She started shouting over and over that Cee Gee Jones was a liar and everyone who worked for her was a liar and liars had to pay. I'm telling you, I was going out of my mind. Everybody in the place was looking at us and all I could think of was what if someone was there who knew Cee Gee or Townie.

"So I got her out on the street. And then she started doing all these cheerleader moves. I mean, she's doing the jumps and split-kicks up and down Lexington Avenue. And I can't stop her . . ."

For the first time I was developing a fondness for Peggy Lawton.

"And all the time she's chanting this weird little poem at the top of her lungs. I'm freaking out and she's chanting and— "

"What?"

"Huh?"

"What was she chanting?"

"She'd go, 'Harry Gay, gotta pay. You will, someday.' Then she'd jump up in the air and—"

"Could it have been Carrie?" I broke in. He looked at me blankly. "The name—could it have been Carrie Gaye instead of Harry?"

He thought for a beat; then he gave me an accommodating smile. "Sure, why not? It could have been Carrie Gaye."

36

After David left, I hung around waiting for Samantha until it became clear that she wasn't coming. Feeling put out—and maybe just a little worried about where the hell she was—I headed back to the studio.

The damn reporters were still camped outside the building. As I was trying to gear myself up for a run on the front entrance, someone grabbed my arm.

"Hi," said Samantha, who seemed to have disguised herself as a bag person—although she might have been following the latest fashion trend for her age group.

"Samantha? I've been leaving messages for you—"

"I know."

"We've got to talk. There's a coffee shop near here . . ."

"Yeah, I know it. It's called Botulism Is Us. I'll buy you a drink. There's a bar over on Tenth Avenue that used to be one of my hangouts."

"It's much too early for a drink, and how do you know about bars on Tenth Avenue at your age?"

She looked at me in astonishment. "Jesus, Angie, I've had a fake ID since I was twelve."

I hate it when I reveal my naïveté to the younger generation.

But Samantha didn't seem to notice. "Angie, you said you

wanted everything I have. Well, you will not believe the shit I found out about Margaret Mae Mapes."

So I let a sixteen-year-old kid drag me to a bar at eleven-thirty in the morning. Excuse me, she was almost seventeen.

The Pub was one of the few old-time working-class bars left on the West Side. It featured clean white-and-black-tile floors and corned beef sandwiches which smelled terrific. Samantha gave me some of hers and for the first time in my life I considered starting an exercise program. The last few days had been wild, calorically speaking, and I could feel the corned beef joining the Moo Shu Pork, apple pie, and stollen on my hips. What scared me was, I was starting to remember how much fun it was to eat things like stollen, apple pie, corned beef, and anything Chinese.

"This had better be good," I said after we'd been served the sandwich and my coffee. Samantha pulled out a pack of cigarettes. "Don't start," she said. "I don't have to," I replied, and gestured to the No Smoking sign. She sighed and put the pack away. "Okay," she said. "First, you've got to promise that you won't give me a lot of shit because I didn't tell your detective pal the truth last night, even though you were sending me fucking hand signals to do it."

"She is well aware that you were lying through your teeth."

"Don't I have a right to protect my sources?"

"Only if you're a journalist. And then they can send you to jail."

"That sucks. Are you sure?"

"I used to watch *Lou Grant* faithfully every Monday night. Now talk to me. Start by explaining how you came up with Ms. Mapes's name."

"Well, after I told you I'd make those calls down to Macon
I started thinking, and I remembered there was this old crock
down there who used to clean the studio. He gave me a toy
whistle he carved and I used to send him Christmas cards after
we left the place. And a couple of times he sent me one. I
used to save letters I got when I was little—so I could play at
having fan mail like Mama. And I put the shit in scrapbooks
like hers. So I found one of the books and sure enough there
was his name. Then I called the station and finally I found this
lady who was a secretary when he still worked there and she
told me where he was."

"Sammy, that's brilliant."

"Shit," she protested. But she was beaming. "Anyway, this
old guy is living with his daughter in North Carolina now, but
he remembered Mama and the show and the name of the
woman who was the guest because he used to know her family."

"So you called him. Good work, Sammy. I am so impressed." We amateur sleuths have to stick together. "Did you
find out where Margaret Mae went after she was on the show?"

"I did better than that."

"You have more?" I was not only impressed, I was getting
a little jealous.

"I called the old crock back this morning, because by the
time I got your message last night it was too late. I'll tell you
the truth, I was so fucking blown away when I found him that
I forgot most of the shit I was supposed to ask him. But when
he got on the phone he was real pissed off. He didn't even
want to talk to me because he thought I'd sicced the reporters
on him."

"What reporters?"

"That's what I asked. Seems some woman who said she

was a reporter from New York called him last night and started driving him loony tunes. He's a grouchy old cocksucker and all he wanted to do was get rid of her. So guess what he told her?" Samantha paused for dramatic effect. I played along.

"What?"

"He told the reporter, or whoever she was, she should talk to Margaret Mae's sister Martha Mae, who moved up north to New Jersey." She paused to take a sip of my coffee. "Can you believe those fucking names?"

"Samantha . . ."

"Okay, okay. Now get this. The sister's full name is Martha Mae Lawton."

37

I don't do as well on four hours' sleep as I used to. I know that's why it took me almost a full minute to put together the fact that Peggy is a nickname for Margaret with the fact that Margaret Mae Mapes had had a daughter who would have been just about Peggy's age. Samantha was a couple of beats ahead of me. "So Peggy was the little bitch who stayed with us down in Georgia," she said. "But if Peggy is Margaret's daughter, why isn't her last name Mapes? Her aunt's name is Lawton. So what the fuck is going on?"

What indeed?

"Where does the aunt live in New Jersey?" I asked.

"My old crock didn't say. But I thought of that too."

"Thought of what?"

"Going to see her, of course."

"That was the farthest thing from my mind," I lied hastily.

"Then why did you ask?" Samantha was a lot sharper at that moment than I was.

"It doesn't make any difference. We don't know where the woman lives, so forget it. I've got to get back to the studio."

Things had been moving quickly in my absence. The ever-informed Cindy cornered me when I got off the elevator. I had the feeling she'd been lying in wait. "Nobody knows what's going on," she complained sotto voce. "We think the police found something in Peggy's desk—she never came back to clear it out. Can you believe that? Anyway, we don't know what they found. Sara's sure she saw one of the detectives put something small into a plastic bag."

"My, that's interesting," I said, and tried to make a break for my office. I wanted to be alone with my thoughts.

"But no one will tell us anything," Cindy went on in an aggrieved tone.

"Uh-huh," I said, and made a feint to the left. No way I was getting rid of Cindy that easily. She did a Hail Mary run around me that positioned her at my side.

"Then after they put the small thing in the plastic bag, your friend, the redheaded policeperson with the fabulous skin, went into Townie's office and they talked for sixteen minutes and twenty-three seconds. After she came out, all the cops left the building. So before I die of curiosity, what's going on?"

"You want *me* to tell *you*? Cindy, I've been out of the office for the last hour and a half."

"Yes, but we've heard all about you. You're in with the police. You're practically one of them. So what gives?"

We'd reached my office and it was clear that she had every intention of coming in with me. "You've got to believe me, I am not 'in with the police' . . ." I began, but Cindy held up her hand in a manner which meant either she was about to do an aria from *Die Walküre,* or she wanted silence. I figured the latter. Sure enough, after I stopped talking, we could hear the muffled sound of a phone ringing in Townie's office next door.

"Come on," Cindy commanded as she raced into my office. She went to the phone on my desk and watched as one of the buttons lit up, indicating that someone in the other office had picked up. She pushed the same button on my phone and reached for the receiver.

"You can't listen in on a private conversation," I whispered, shocked.

"Pooh!" Cindy whispered back. "Townie does it to everyone, all the time." She picked up the phone and began eavesdropping, while I mouthed useless things like "Put it down" and "You can't do this." Finally I took the receiver from her—and then had to give it back because I was afraid I'd make too much noise hanging up.

She did the honors expertly. And in the nick of time because the red light on the phone went off seconds later. That delicate mission accomplished, she turned to me triumphantly.

"Sara was right," she crowed. "Your friend the detective did find something in Peggy's desk. It was a cassette tape."

I wish I could say I am of such strong moral fiber that I gave her a stern lecture, refused to hear more, and sent her on her way. Failing that, I wish at least I'd had several minutes of deeply wrenching struggle with my conscience before I said, "Tell me every word they said." But I didn't.

Cindy gave me a smile that told me my ethics were gurgling down the tube along with my diet, and said, "Your police friend asked a lot of questions about editing audio and lifting the sound portion from videotapes, and could a good editor put together a cassette tape that would sound like a real person talking? Especially if it was recorded on another device. Townie told her it could. And then your detective said she assumed that anyone who had access to the building could get ahold of videotapes of the show and Townie said yes, and that was when you took the phone away from me," she ended on a note of reproach. I ignored it. My weary mind was too busy digesting what she'd said and trying to figure out what to do next. In spite of what I'd told Samantha, a trip to New Jersey was clearly indicated. If I just knew where to go.

"So what does it all mean?" Cindy demanded.

"I don't know," I said. I forced my brain to function. It lurched into action unwillingly, but it came up with a plan.

"I guess Peggy will have a lot of explaining to do when she gets back from New Jersey," I said casually. Cindy jumped on the tidbit.

"Is that where she went? Because the police were asking and no one could say for sure."

I shrugged. "Where else would she go? Where does that aunt of hers live again? Fort Lee?"

"I thought it was Lincoln Park."

"Oh yes, that's right. Isn't that dumb, dumb, dumb? I'm the one who has the aunt in Fort Lee."

Cindy didn't care. "About the tape . . ." she prodded. My phone buzzed and I jumped guiltily. Cindy, I noted with chagrin, did not.

It was Felice. "Angie? Could you come into Cee Gee's office, please?"

I headed for the door fast.

"But you haven't told me what all this stuff means," Cindy wailed.

"I haven't a clue," I said over my shoulder.

I think I ruined her day.

38

When I walked into the office, all three of them were
there—Townie, Felice, and Cee Gee—sitting together the way
they had on the night I'd first met them. But the feeling was
now very different. Cee Gee was upright on the sofa. Felice
sat near the window and looked out at the river. Only Townie's shoes were off. She sat in a large chair with her feet tucked
up under her.

"Angie, we want you to make an announcement that we're
closing down before one o'clock today," said Townie. "I'm
afraid we have some very sad news. We don't know exactly
why, but it looks as if Peggy Lawton is going to be arrested
for the murder of Grace Shipley."

She looked positively radiant.

I called New Jersey information from the public booth in the
lobby and got the number for Martha Mae Lawton. Who was not
home in Lincoln Park. But her daughter, Melinda Mae, was.
And she was thrilled to hear that she was one of five finalists in
a contest for a date with the actor who played Dirk Tarrow on
Bright Tomorrow, although she couldn't imagine who might
have submitted her name. And yes, she would love to meet a
representative from the show. However, she couldn't do it a

home because her mom was kind of funny about how much television she watched. And anyway, she added with belated caution, she wasn't sure she should let strangers into the house. I understood her position and we agreed to meet in the food court at the Willowbrook Mall as soon as I could get out to New Jersey. Melinda Mae would be wearing a white shirt with blue flowers on it and red cowboy boots.

What Melinda Mae neglected to tell me was that she weighed well over two hundred pounds. And that the poppies were an amorphous mass of blue studs which had been applied to a T-shirt by loving hands at home. If it hadn't been for the red boots I'd never have found her. She was seated in front of a pile of goodies which included a stuffed baked potato, a burrito, a taco, two slices of pizza, a couple of outsized chocolate chip cookies, and a frozen yogurt.

"This is my lunch," she said after I'd introduced myself as Lucy Stone, director of special events for *Bright Tomorrow*. A small puddle of her yogurt had melted onto her pizza. Or maybe it was the sour cream from her potato. It didn't seem to matter much as she crammed down half the slice.

"You want something?" she inquired through a mouthful of cheese and tomato.

"Perhaps a little coffee," I said faintly, and moved to one of the food court counters to get some.

"We have a tiny problem," I said after I'd settled down and she'd returned from a repeat visit to the frozen yogurt bar. "The rules of our contest say you're ineligible if any member of your family works in the television industry."

"No problemo. Nobody does. Tell me about Dirk. Is he that sexy in real life?"

Actually, the actor's name was Steve Robbe and all I could tell her about his love life was that his longtime live-in, Bruce, seemed like a happy man.

"But I'm afraid you do have a cousin who works in the industry. Her name is Peggy Lawton."

"Crazy Peggy? You gotta be kidding. I mean, I haven't seen her in years, but I can't believe it. It's gotta be another Peggy."

"This Peggy Lawton works for Cee Gee Jones."

"Now I know you got the wrong person. Peggy always hated Cee Gee."

"You mean she hates the show?"

"No, she hates Cee Gee Jones. She thinks Cee Gee killed her mother."

39

"See, my aunt Margaret was a guest on Cee Gee Jones's show when she was living down south. She came up here afterward because she wanted to get into acting. My mom always said that show put the idea in her head—Mom is born-again, and ever since Jim and Tammy Faye went down, she thinks television is the work of Satan." She laughed loudly. Unfortunately, she hadn't quite finished swallowing her last dollop of frozen yogurt.

"Why would Peggy have such an absurd idea about Cee Gee Jones? How could she possibly believe Cee Gee was responsible for her mother's death?"

"Because my aunt Margaret was murdered by one of her boyfriends and Peggy had to blame it on someone. Aunt Margaret was always on the wild side," she added a touch wistfully. "Guys gave her money and things. That's what Mom said, 'cause Aunt Margaret never worked and she and Peggy always had plenty. Until Aunt Margaret was killed."

"But why accuse Ms. Jones?"

"Peggy said her mom knew some deep dark secret about Cee Gee Jones. 'Cause they never found the guy who killed Aunt Margaret, so Peggy just got this idea in her head. But Peggy's crazy. I mean, she's really nuts—been in the hospital once and everything. You're not going to let her stop me in the contest, are you?"

"Well, the rules are very clear . . ."

"That's not fair."

"Perhaps if I understood a little more about your cousin's obsession with Ms. Jones . . ." Which made absolutely no sense, but Melinda Mae Lawton was not in a mood to question it. A potent combination of fantasy and lust was blocking her ability to think logically. Steve Robbe often has that effect on his devoted following.

"Peggy was only six years old when her mom was killed, okay?" said Melinda. "My mom did everything she could for Peggy. My parents even adopted her. Then when she was about eighteen, she started all this stuff about Cee Gee Jones. I'm telling you she's like that guy who went ape over Jodie Foster and tried to kill the president." Then, afraid she might have hurt her own case, she added, "But I'm completely different from Peggy. I don't even like her. I never see her. Please don't kick me out of the contest."

"I'll see what I can do," I promised.

Back in the city I went straight to the precinct, but Teresa was gone. I spoke to Hank, who could not—or would not—tell me where she was. However, she had left a message for me. Which he delivered, although I could tell it went against the grain to discuss a case with a civilian. "Teresa wanted you to know that we found a black canvas garment bag at Ms. Lawton's apartment."

"Does it match the fibers in the doll's hair?"

"Yes," he said stiffly.

"What about the other things—the heart, and the book? Was Peggy responsible for them?"

"My instructions from Teresa were to tell you about the garment bag—that's all."

"But—"

"I really can't say any more, Ms. DaVito. You'll probably hear about it all soon enough," he added grimly. I thought I heard him add under his breath, "Stupid son of a bitch." However, by that point I was so tired I could have been hallucinating.

Not that I got any sleep when I went home. Because Hank was right. The final chapter in the story of the murder had exploded. And I got it, along with the rest of America, via television.

The first mention came late that afternoon on the twenty-four-hour local New York news channel.

A young anchor, fresh out of journalism school, looked intently into the camera. "Police announced a breakthrough in what newspapers here are calling the 'Cee Gee Killing,'" he said. A trace of Long Island still hovered around his consonants; I hoped he was working on it with a speech coach. "Discovery of vital new evidence has brought them close to solving this case, according to Detective Phil Mariceaux of the NYPD."

There was a close-up of the detective I'd seen with Hank and Teresa. He was a vision in plaid. In his eyes was the classic deer-in-the-headlights look of the camera-phobic. Television was not his métier.

"As I understand it, Detective," said an off-camera interviewer, "one of the big questions in this case has been, how did the murderer manage to convince Grace Shipley to go to Cee Gee Jones's apartment?"

"Yes," said Phil.

"Ms. Jones's doorman has said that the victim, Grace Shipley, told him she was there for a meeting with Ms. Jones at Ms. Jones's invitation."

"Yes," said Phil.

"Ms. Shipley said she found a message from Ms. Jones on her answering machine—is that true, Detective?" The interviewer was starting to sound desperate.

"Yes," said Phil.

"But now we understand that you have discovered a cleverly doctored tape of Cee Gee Jones's voice which may have been used by the real murderer."

"Yes," said Phil.

"And this tape was found in the desk of this suspect?"

"Yes," said Phil.

"Fascinating," said the interviewer with some asperity. "Thank you, Detective."

"Yes," said Phil.

The august anchor of the nation's top-rated news show read his TelePrompTer gravely. "The final chapter was played out today in the murder of talk show hostess Cee Gee Jones's longtime associate Grace Shipley. Police now have an arrest warrant out for an office worker in Ms. Jones's organization named Peggy Lawton . . ." A grainy picture of Peggy standing behind Cee Gee at some function involving flowers and trophies flashed on the screen. "Lawton has a long history of mental problems which probably began with the murder of her mother when she was six . . ."

The two reporters on *Inside Info* were ecstatic. "This is one weird story, Beryl," gloated Dick. "It seems that Peggy Lawton was the daughter of a woman who was a guest on a talk show Cee Gee Jones did in Georgia in the early eighties. The woman's name was Margaret Mae Mapes . . ."

The natty Britisher on *Hard Story* oozed sympathy. "Margaret Mae Mapes was shot and killed in a New Jersey motel room very much like this one," he droned, over footage of a sleazy bedroom. I was willing to bet his show had miles of stock footage featuring motel bedrooms in various degrees of sleaze. "Margaret Mae Mapes left the South devastated by her experience on a talk show hosted by then unknown Cee Gee Jones . . ." That wasn't exactly the way Melinda Mae told it, but what the hell. "With her young daughter she moved north to be near her sister Martha and to start a new life. That new life was cut short horribly . . ."

"The killer of Margaret Mae Mapes was never found." The hostess of *Happening Today* flashed a beauty pageant smile at all of us out in television land. "That tragedy seems to have unhinged the mind of her young daughter, Margaret, also known as Peggy. Peggy was sent to live with her aunt Martha Mae Lawton. Martha Mae told us in an exclusive 'News Now' interview that young Peggy always blamed talk show superstar Cee Gee Jones for the death of her mother, Margaret Mae Mapes."

The camera came up on a woman clutching a bag of groceries in front of a Shop Rite supermarket. She was an older and chubbier version of Melinda Mae. Clearly this was the born-again mother. "Am I on?" she asked someone off camera. Presumably she got the nod, because she looked into the lens with remarkable poise and said gravely, "Peggy always blamed Cee Gee Jones for her mama's death." It seemed that Martha Mae had gotten over her aversion to the devil tube.

The very blond and chic female reporter who had recently moved to "News Now" from a classier morning show was indignant. "Cee Gee Jones has been a guest in my home," she stated firmly to her male cohort, "and I'm here to tell you that she had nothing to do with the death of Margaret Mae Mapes, a woman whose life touched hers briefly but dramatically in the early eighties. The truth is that Margaret Mae Mapes was a party girl, to put it kindly, with a history of violent relationships with men. We spoke with her sister, Martha Mae Lawton, in this exclusive interview from her home in New Jersey."

Martha Mae was learning fast. For this appearance her hair was pulled off her face, and she'd put on lipstick. She was posed on a couch in front of a large portrait of Elvis. "Lord forgive me for speaking ill of my own sister, but Margaret Mae had turned her back on salvation," she said with great feeling. "She gave men her favors and she took money for them. I wasn't surprised when I heard she had gone the way she did. The vengeance of the Lord is mighty and He works in His own ways. I prayed for Maggie Mae. And now I got to pray for

Peggy, too." In spite of the tears which had started flowing, I thought she seemed absolutely delighted.

"You've got this lady Peggy Lawton who thinks Cee Gee Jones murdered her mother, Margaret Mae Mapes," said the comedian who was trying to resuscitate his career on a late-night talk show. "Now at the time when Margaret Mae Mapes was killed in New Jersey, Cee Gee Jones was in New York in a television studio taping her show. In front of one hundred and fifty people. But still, Peggy Lawton believes Cee Gee Jones did it. Hello? Earth to Peggy? Have too many cousins been marrying cousins in that family tree, or what?"

The phone rang before I could find something to throw at the set.

"Angie, it's all so fucking terrific, isn't it?" For the first time since I'd known her, Samantha sounded bubbly.

"I'm glad it worked out the way you wanted, Sammy."

"Mama's having a brunch on New Year's Day. It's gonna be real small because of all the shit that's happened, but they wanted me to ask you to come."

It was the last thing I wanted to do.

"I may be busy . . ."

"Oh." There was no mistaking her disappointment. "Well, if you've got something better to do I understand . . . I just thought we could hang out."

What the hell.

"I'd love to come."

———

I managed to resist the lure of the tube for almost two hours. I turned it on again for the late-night news roundup.

The two interchangeable female anchors rehashed the story point by weary point. "Police say they now have proof that it was Peggy Lawton who sent several gruesome items to Cee Gee Jones," said Clarice to Janine—or it may have been Janine telling Clarice. Pictures of the heart with the bullet in it, the book with the death certificate, and the Cee Gee doll appeared on the screen. The stuff looked much more ominous in the enhanced-for-TV color blowups than it had in real life. "A search of Ms. Lawton's apartment on the Lower East Side of Manhattan turned up this trunk," Janine—or Clarice—continued over a shot of a flowered toy chest. "In it detectives found a child's game from which the plastic heart was taken, several copies of Cee Gee Jones's autobiography, surgical gloves, and a typewriter. They are speculating that all of this was used by Ms. Lawton when she put together those macabre artifacts." The women closed the show by reporting that there was no word of an arrest. However, they speculated that a search for Peggy Lawton was probably under way at that very moment. They urged viewers to stay tuned, then signed off, their smiles again bright.

40

By the time I woke up the next morning, the pundits and the talking heads and the experts had all handed down their verdict: In her craziness, Peggy Lawton had killed Grace Shipley. Prominent psychologists acting as consultants to the various networks theorized that it had been her plan to kill off all of Cee Gee's inner circle before killing Cee Gee herself. Displaced anger, they said. And projection.

At ten o'clock I went to Freddie's apartment so he could show me for the millionth time how to water his plants and feed his cat, who hates me. This is yet another of our rituals. Every New Year's Eve, Freddie and his significant other trek out to their beach house on Fire Island. And every time Freddie leaves me in charge of his home, he has to give me instructions on the care and feeding of the African violets and Ethel Merman. Who is known as "the Merm" to her friends. Of whom I am not one. Her choice, not mine.

"Want me to take your phone messages, or are you going to risk the remote?" I asked. Freddie has not trusted the remote since the time it malfunctioned and erased messages from both the Coast and his mother.

"Don't you dare touch that phone," he yelped. "I've got the

call forwarding programmed for this little baby." He patted his flip phone fondly.

"Can you do that?" For some reason it disturbed me.

"This phone can do anything. Why are you looking like that?"

"Technology," I said vaguely. "Do you realize they're re-organizing the genetic makeup of the tomatoes you eat?"

"Angie, I worry about you. If you're not careful you're going to start running around picketing companies that make computer chips."

The Merm emerged from hiding to hiss at me. I considered it a mark of maturity that I didn't hiss back. But I was starting to get depressed.

By evening I was mildly suicidal. I told myself it had nothing to do with the fact that it was New Year's Eve and Patrick had not called to claim the raincheck.

Meanwhile Peggy haunted me. I felt responsible for her. It was not a logical way to feel, but then it had been that kind of week. And I certainly had sent the ball rolling in her direction. What if she hadn't killed Grace Shipley? The case against Peggy was strong. But the case against Cee Gee had also been strong. Peggy had a motive; so did Cee Gee. Peggy did not have an alibi for the time of the murder; neither did Cee Gee. There was one piece of evidence that seemed to tip the scales toward Peggy—the cassette tape found in her desk. But why did Peggy leave it in her desk at the studio? Why not keep it home with the rest of the junior terrorist kit in the flowered trunk?

And why had Teresa taken off right after they found that crucial bit of evidence.

———

Connie called at eleven-thirty to wish me Happy New Year and tell me she wished I was there. The whole family was making resolutions and drinking a spiced punch they'd made from a recipe in her Merrye Olde England cookbook. I wished her Happy New Year and was glad I was miles away from Connecticut.

At five minutes to twelve, I called Patrick to wish him Happy New Year. It was not a big deal, I told myself. It was just a friendly, spontaneous little call—which I practiced for fifteen minutes. He was out. Of course. He had plans for New Year's Eve. Everyone in the civilized world had plans for New Year's Eve except me. I left my witty, lighthearted message on Patrick's answering machine. The swine.

Not that I wanted plans. I hate New Year's Eve. It's a fake holiday tacked onto the end of the Christmas season because nobody's ready to face January yet. Besides, I could have had plans for New Year's Eve if I had wanted them. I could have gone to my sister's house. I thought with a shudder about my last bus trip up to Connecticut, on Christmas Eve Day. I dwelt particularly on young Lexy, who kept getting greener and greener as the bus made its slow, torturous way up to New Milford. With my luck, I thought, if I'd gone to Connie's for New Year's Eve, there would have been another traffic-stopping accident just because I was on the bus. The thought of another trip lasting three hours, forty-two minutes, and eighteen seconds was enough to send me to bed.

That night I had black, angry dreams. The kind I never remember because I don't want to.

41

I didn't remember my dreams, but the heaviness was still with me when I woke up to greet the new year. And I had the feeling that there was something I knew, but wasn't putting together. I tried forcing myself to focus on whatever it was, but my mind won't work that way. My usual MO, mentally speaking, is for my right brain to solve problems when I'm not looking. Then it hits me with an "ah hah" moment when I'm thinking about something else. At best it's an inefficient way to function. At times it can be downright dangerous.

As I rode the elevator up to Cee Gee's apartment for her New Year's Day brunch, I wondered how the general mood would be. Peggy Lawton was the announced suspect in Grace Shipley's murder, but there was still no word on her arrest. The thought of the unhinged girl—guilty or not—walking around the streets was unnerving.

I spotted Cee Gee in the foyer when I walked in. She was wearing a tricky shade of green that made her look tired. Or maybe she really was tired. But if she was anxious about Peggy's whereabouts, she didn't let on. Felice stood next to her, decked in jewels by the pound, while Sammy hovered over her mom protectively. I did a little party wave and Sammy smiled back. There was genuine relief in her eyes.

The party was small. Most of the guests seemed to be *Cee*

Gee! staffers. I knew a few of them well enough to greet, which for some reason made me sad.

Someone passed me something with caviar on it to eat. Someone handed me a flute of champagne. I made my way over to Cee Gee.

"Angie, we've been hoping you'd come," she said. "We were wondering if you've heard anything from your police friend."

"I thought we decided not to talk about that," said Felice, but Cee Gee ignored her.

"Why hasn't there been an arrest?" she asked. "We need closure, Angie. For ourselves and the fans."

"I'm sure Teresa is doing everything she can," I said. There was no reason for me to feel defensive, but I did.

"I'm not complaining—just trying to communicate our needs. So we can begin working on the healing. You see, I feel responsible for all of this."

"Bullshit, Mama," said Sammy. "It's not your fault Peggy's crazy."

"But I always say that my show is my family; I should have been more aware of her pain. We might have been able to help her." She paused to favor us all with a beatific smile. "That's why I've decided that if poor Peggy has to stand trial, I will hire the best lawyer for her that money can buy."

Of course she would. And the story would go out to all the media by sundown.

"And we're going to do a show about people who become fixated on celebrities. We've already managed to sign up Peggy's aunt to be a guest."

That was when I knew I was going to quit this job before I started it. Screw being a pro. I was going to walk out of this white-on-white cave and call Freddie on his ridiculous flip phone in his hot tub or wherever the hell he was on the island and—

And all of a sudden, I had my "ah hah" moment. Right there at brunch. "Take that," said my right brain triumphantly, and strolled away. Leaving me with a solution that was so simple, and so complicated . . . But it made sense. If I could put the pieces together. I forced myself to keep breathing and gave it a whirl.

"It seems like it's been such a long time since Grace was . . ." I began, but I could feel Sammy tighten next to me. "Since everything happened," I amended. "I keep going over that day in my mind. You were delivering food to the shelters, weren't you, Cee Gee?"

"Yes, the way we do every Christmas Eve Day."

"You do it in the morning, right? How long did it take you?"

"We stopped at noon."

And then, according to all the reams of paper and the hundreds of hours of airtime which had been devoted to this story, George dropped Townie and Cee Gee at the studio and took off for the country.

"And after you went to the studio, Townie left to go shopping."

"Yes," said a familiar light voice behind me. "At Pratesi." Townie materialized, followed by George. Well, why not? Now the gang was all here.

"Cee Gee wanted monogrammed linens for her house in the country," Townie went on. "Do you know when she first met me she didn't even know there was such a thing?"

Cee Gee grinned her famous grin. "Townie taught me everything I know," she said.

"It's all been worth it," said Townie. She was holding a glass of champagne. "To our bright and beautiful future," she toasted.

For the first time I saw just how fragile all that pale, chiseled beauty could be. And that was when the pieces really came together.

42

I waited at least another ten minutes before I made my exit and even then I was afraid I might be pushing it. But I had to get out of there. Because I had to talk to Teresa. I tried three times on the street, but the phones all ate my quarters without producing a dial tone. So I headed home fast.

I didn't have the whole picture, but I was pretty sure I had enough. Let Teresa deal with the loose ends. If and when I was able to make contact with Teresa.

I told Rosario to let Detective O'Hanlon in as soon as she arrived, and raced up to my apartment to start phoning. Teresa wasn't at the police station. She wasn't at her home. There was no answer at Patrick's. I left urgent messages. I thought I remembered she'd said something about relatives in Queens. I called information and tried several Gallaghers I picked at random from the phone company. I apologized for the wrong numbers.

I tried to make some coffee but my hands seemed to be shaking. Teresa had no right to do this to me, I raged. She was supposed to be a workaholic, so why wasn't she working? Why the hell wasn't she somewhere I could find her?

I sat by the phone and willed it to ring. Which is why, when

I heard the doorbell, I ran to open the door without thinking. Also, I was trusting Rosario's screening abilities. It may have been the first time in my life I was ever too trusting. I realized my mistake when it was too late.

He was so very dapper.

"May I come in, Angela of Life?" he asked.

"I'm busy . . ."

He pushed past me and closed the door. I hadn't realized how strong he was.

"How . . . How did you get in?" I stammered.

"There is a boy downstairs in your lobby attempting to deliver twelve pizzas to your first-floor neighbor, who did not order them. It has taken your doorman's attention."

"You're good at getting past doormen, aren't you?"

"Always pay attention to the servants, I was trained in my youth."

"Especially little foibles like Al's weakness for the ponies."

"Exactly." He gave me a jaunty little smile, but he looked old and weary. I backed up in the general direction of the door.

"Stand still," he commanded.

He pulled a gun out of the pocket of his beautifully tailored jacket. I decided for once it might be a good thing if I obeyed.

"I've been wondering if you'd ever figure it out, Angela," he said. "And then when I heard you asking Cee Gee when I left for Connecticut, I knew you had."

The gun was pointed at me. It was a small, snub-nosed weapon made out of something that was shiny and silver. And I'd always thought guns were black. I tried not to look at it, but it was mesmerizing. I began to talk. Talking always reassures me.

"It really was very clever the way you set up the alibi for

Townie and yourself," I said, in a voice that didn't shake as badly as I'd thought it would. "The entire Pratesi staff could testify that at the time of the murder Townie was in their store calling you at your house in Connecticut."

He executed a courtly little bow. The gun was still trained on me.

"But you weren't in Connecticut. You were in Cee Gee's apartment waiting for Grace and talking to your wife on a cellular phone. Which was picking up the call that had been forwarded from your house in Connecticut. Very nice."

"Thank you." He was actually enjoying this.

"The timing was particularly well worked out."

"Except for one small detail," he said ruefully.

"But that wasn't your fault."

"How kind of you to say so."

"It's the truth." I was starting to relax—at least enough so that some blood was getting to my brain cells again. Analyzing my predicament was once more an option. The door was behind me, but I was too far away to make a run for it. "You had no way of knowing there would be an accident outside Danbury that would tie up traffic for hours," I went on. "So there was no way you could possibly have made the trip to Kent in time to receive a two o'clock call on that day."

"The gods are not always kind," he murmured. I tried inching toward the door. "Stop that," he snapped.

I froze obediently. He raised the gun slightly so it was pointing exactly at the center of my chest—at least that's the way it seemed from my vantage point. For what seemed like a couple of years we stared at each other. Finally he said, "Do continue, Angela. I'm curious to know just how much you've worked out."

I took a breath. "Peggy Lawton said that Cee Gee's show

was built on a scam. She was talking about her mother's role in the early stages of it. Margaret Mae Mapes was never in any danger, was she? But after her first appearance on the show, Cee Gee got so much attention they had to keep the story going. So they staged a little shoot-'em-up outside Margaret's house."

"Actually, they never had to go that far. A well-told story and two shots fired into the front door sufficed."

"Who did the shooting?"

He hesitated, but just for a second. "When Victoria was a young girl, her father used to take her skeet shooting."

I nodded. It confirmed what I'd already suspected. "And then they paid Margaret Mae to go along with the hoax," I said.

"They paid her an arm and a leg."

"And then they paid her again to leave town. Because when she went north she had money."

"She had plenty."

"But when Cee Gee hit it big in New York, Margaret Mae came back for more. She threatened to go public with the hoax. She blackmailed them."

"She was a greedy piece of work, the late Ms. Mapes."

"And Townie was smart enough to realize that something had to be done or they'd never be rid of her."

Now the fun was over for him. The words hit him and he blinked. And I gained six inches on the door.

"So Townie killed her," I said softly.

He stared at me. Ramrod-straight back. Eyes that wanted to weep. But he didn't do that sort of thing.

"You must think you're very clever, Angela," he said softly.

"Not really. For a while I toyed with the idea that you might have killed Margaret. But you hate Cee Gee and her show. If anything you were probably rooting for Margaret Mae to bring her down."

"That show was the worst thing that ever happened to Victoria."

The door was still out of reach. But the hand that was holding the gun wasn't quite as steady as it had been. Emotion was taking its toll on George.

"Did Townie tell you what she'd done right away, George?" I asked gently.

"That night. She always tells me everything." Oddly, there was a kind of pride and love in the way he said it. "Grace covered for her in the control booth. Vicky met Margaret in the motel room and . . ."

"Killed her," I finished for him. "Did Felice know?"

He shook his head. "She hadn't joined the show yet. She knew about the hoax down in Georgia—they told her that. But that was all."

"What about Cee Gee? Did she know?"

"She was never told. But she knew. Not that she'd ever admit it even to herself. She let Vicky live with it. All these years. But in her gut the hypocritical little bitch has always known."

"So then when Cee Gee fired Grace, Grace put the pressure on Townie. I heard her threaten Townie one day."

"So did I. Many times. And Cee Gee let my Vicky twist in the wind."

"And then Peggy started planting her crazy presents, and everyone except Townie figured it was Grace threatening Cee Gee with the old story about the scam. But Townie thought the warning was meant for her."

He nodded. He'd lowered the gun slightly—his arm had to

be tired. But he was watching me too closely for another move to the door.

"It was the toy bullets," he said wearily. "Vicky was sure Grace was using them to send a message."

"So Townie tried to keep Cee Gee from firing Grace, but Cee Gee was too angry. And after so much time she was willing to risk that her public would forgive her if Grace told the story of the hoax."

He nodded again; it was as if he was too exhausted to talk.

"Townie was in an unbelievable bind," I went on, like a demented professor giving a lecture to a class of one. "If she didn't save Grace's job, Grace threatened to tell the authorities about the murder of Margaret Mae. But Cee Gee was insistent on firing Grace. Finally Townie decided there was only one thing she could do . . ."

"Yes," he said in whisper. "She decided."

"Again."

He nodded. The gun lowered maybe another inch.

"And you knew Townie was going to kill Grace."

He looked past me at some happier time I couldn't see. I made a tiny move toward the door.

"I wish you had known Vicky before she met that piece of white trash," he said softly. I moved some more.

"She was such a glorious girl—beautiful, and eager, and so full of life. I fell in love with her the first time I saw her."

I could almost reach the doorknob.

"It was at my daughter's deb party. Such a farce really. An old fool at a silly party falling in love with a girl half his age who was dressed in white. But I had to have her."

"And now you've become a murderer for her sake. You tried to set it up so that Cee Gee would be blamed. You knew you'd need a little luck for that, but you don't mind relying on luck. You're a gambler. Except when it comes to Townie."

"I couldn't let her kill Grace. I couldn't let her do it again."

"So you did it for her."

Fatigue and emotional pain got the better of him. In spite of his self-control he had to brush his eyes. I grabbed the doorknob and tried to turn it. But the gun was back in position in a flash, its nasty little snub nose gleaming at me.

"Let go of the knob, and walk away from the door," he commanded. But at that moment an unearthly scream came from the wall behind me. It was followed by the static from hell.

It threw him. Just for a few seconds, but it was enough for me to finish opening the door, and slam it behind me. I heard the click of the self-lock and breathed a sigh of relief. Then I remembered that the lock kept people out of the apartment, not in it.

I ran for the elevator as I heard him open the door. I had a jump on him because I knew the ins and outs of the hallway—unfortunately, the gun gave him the bigger jump. By the time I reached the elevator he was still behind me, but gaining fast.

"Please let the damn fucking door open," I prayed to the god of mechanical devices. For once in my life prayer worked. The door opened and I threw myself into the car as I heard an explosion behind me.

"Angie, what the hell . . . ?" said a familiar voice.

"Patrick?" There was a second shot and the doors closed because he was pushing the down button frantically. But for some reason he was sitting on the floor and reaching up to do it. It didn't seem a good time to point out to him that he was getting his beautiful Armani tux dirty.

"Patrick, what—"

"You called me. Sounded crazy." The elevator began its downward trip with a mighty lurch. For some reason Patrick winced.

"You made Rosario use the intercom," I babbled. "You saved me." Then I noticed the patch of red that was growing rapidly on his exquisite right sleeve. He was very, very white. "Oh my God, Patrick . . ."

"I've always hated stories about damsels in distress," he said through gritted teeth. Then he passed out.

Epilogue

"You fainted, Shortstuff," said Teresa. "You never could stand the sight of blood."

"Damnit, Teresa, I was shot and I passed out."

"It was just a flesh wound."

They'd been going at it ever since Teresa arrived at Patrick's apartment. He was stretched out on the couch looking adorable. At least I thought so. Thanks to a hefty dose of painkillers he didn't seem too much the worse for his ordeal, and Teresa was trying to pretend she hadn't been worried sick when she heard he was shot.

"How would you know what kind of wound it was?" he demanded. "You weren't there when they stitched me up. Angie took me to the emergency room."

"I had a bad guy to capture."

Actually, capturing George had not been difficult. My downstairs neighbors heard the shots and called 911. George was in the hallway outside my apartment when the cops found him, and he turned himself in without a murmur. Teresa was informed of the shooting while she was in Cee Gee's apartment questioning Townie about the murder of Margaret Mae Mapes. When Townie heard about George she made a full confession.

"What made you suspect Townie in Margaret Mae's death?" I asked Teresa.

"You were the one who started me thinking. It was when you said Peggy Lawton was one of those people no one ever believes even when they're absolutely right. If I accepted the idea that Peggy was right about her mother knowing a potentially damaging secret about Cee Gee Jones, then Margaret Mae's unsolved murder became too much of a coincidence.

"Ms. Jones couldn't have killed Margaret Mae because Ms. Jones was on camera at the time of the murder. Since Ms. Rovere had not yet joined the show, that left Ms. Shipley and Ms. Townsend-Stuart."

"And since Ms. Shipley is now defunct, that leaves one little Indian named Townie. Let's hear it for Sherlock O'Hanlon and her faithful Angie, Watson . . . 'Scuse me—Watson, Angie," said Patrick, whose painkillers were obviously starting to kick in big-time.

"What about the cassette in Peggy's drawer?" I asked.

"I knew it was a plant. Hank and I had already gone through that desk. But Detective Mariceaux felt the need to see for himself. He thought perhaps we might not have been thorough enough."

From the couch Patrick gave Mariceaux and his doubts about Teresa's efficiency a loud, drawn-out Bronx cheer.

"When he found the tape, Detective Mariceaux was convinced that he'd solved the case. He and the captain decided to divulge the information to the press." Teresa paused and a small smile tugged at the corner of her mouth. "I suggested that it should be Detective Mariceaux who made the public announcement."

"Did you catch that poor son of bitch on television? Teresa let him hang himself," crowed her proud brother.

"It was unfortunate that he was premature in his announcement," said Teresa blandly.

"She's just like the old man," Patrick raved. "He pulled the same thing on a hot-shit rookie back in sixty-four . . ."

"I'm sure Detective Mariceaux hasn't done his career any permanent damage," said Teresa.

Maybe not, but the look in her eyes said he wasn't going to have an easy time of it for a while. I looked at her with new respect.

"How did the tape get in Peggy's desk?" I asked.

"It seems that Ms. Townsend-Stuart overheard the receptionist at the studio tell you you had a call from Samantha Jones. That whetted her curiosity. So she went to her office, waited until you dialed what she thought was Samantha's number, and eavesdropped."

"And she heard me talking to the librarian at Lincoln Center Library."

"At which point she discovered that Peggy Lawton had an unusual interest in the early days of Cee Gee Jones's career. Since she was pretty sure Ms. Lawton had also sabotaged Ms. Jones's alibi, she was afraid that Ms. Lawton might have some axe to grind, perhaps in connection with the fate of Margaret Mae Mapes. So she made a few phone calls."

The way Sammy had. So she also tracked down the old janitor, who told her about Martha Mae Lawton.

"So that was how she found out who Peggy was," I said. "Where did she get the tape?"

"Ms. Townsend-Stuart suspected from the beginning that it was her husband who killed Ms. Shipley. When she decided to frame Ms. Lawton, she confronted him and he confessed. He gave her the tape he had made by lifting the audio portion of videos of Cee Gee Jones. It was the tape which Ms. Shipley heard on her answering machine."

And it became the piece of evidence Townie used to implicate Peggy in her attempt to bail out both her husband and Cee Gee.

A snore from the couch explained why we hadn't heard from Patrick in a while. His medication had finally gotten the better of him.

"I wonder what will happen to Peggy," I whispered.

"She may actually have a chance to have a life now. It would probably help if she talked to a professional. I thought I might try to see her in a day or two and suggest it. What about Ms. Jones? Will her show be ruined by this?"

"Are you kidding? Cee Gee will find a way to turn this into the biggest publicity bonanza of her career."

"How will she get along without Ms. Townsend-Stuart?"

"Cee Gee will always find a producer to take care of her. As a matter of fact I think she's got one of the best potential producer/caretakers ever waiting in the wings right now."

"Ms. Rovere?"

"Sammy. She was born for it."

"Pity. The child would have made a wonderful cop."

Another snore from the sleeping beauty on the couch reminded me of one last question which I had decided would go unanswered for the moment—it was a two-parter.

I wanted to know where the hell Patrick had been the night before and why the hell he was still wearing his dress clothes when he showed up at my apartment the next day.

I figured I'd wait until his stitches were out before I asked him about it, though. After all, I'd seen the look on his face when the doctor in the emergency room had to cut the sleeve of his beautiful tux to get it off him. The man had suffered well and truly at that moment. Which served him right if he'd been wearing that tux for someone female who wasn't his mother. Even if he did save my life. But I was going to cut him some slack.

I thought that showed great maturity.